Beth,

Ei

GIFT OF GRACE

Many Blessings,
Lynette Eason
Prov. 3:5-6

Lynette Eason

Author Acknowledgements

M any thanks to my wonderful, patient, and supportive husband, Jack. You are everything I ever dreamed of having in a husband and then some. God has truly blessed me! I love you more. Thank you to my precious children, Lauryn and Will for understanding when I told them, "In a minute." I thank my family – extended as well as immediate – for your love and support. More specifically, I'm so grateful to my parents, Lewis and Lou Jean Barker, for raising me in a Christian home and being a Godly example of what it means to love unconditionally. A big thanks goes to my brother, Lane, for providing the original computer on which I started writing - and all the technical support necessary! Hi to my Grandma, Freda Trowbridge, in Amarillo, Texas. Thanks so much for encouraging me and loving me long distance. To my in-laws, Bill and Diane Eason, who've taken me in as one of their own. I love you much.

Carolyn Rice, thank you for being such an encourager. I appreciate our friendship. You're the one who needs to write a book!

Thanks go out to Northgate Baptist: my friends and co-workers at the South Carolina School for the Deaf and Blind – Becky, Tracy, Cindy, Loreta, Cathy, Dana, Sarah, Sally, Debbie B. and Scott – just to name a few! I'd go nuts without your shoulders to cry on and laugh therapy sessions to get me through the day.

Jesse Hartley, thanks for the constructive criticism and belief in Grace. See you next year at Ridgecrest. Thank you Preacher Roger and Carol Plemmons for your enthusiasm and friendship. Thank you, also, Roger, for preaching the word of God unapologetically and boldly. Preach on! But most of all, I thank you God for your precious son, Jesus Christ and all that He sacrificed for me. I love you with my whole heart. This book is for you!

Prologue

Grace bounced slightly in her auditorium seat causing a blond curl to drop across one intent blue eye. An impatient hand swept it back. She was listening to the man up front talk about Jesus. He was saying that Jesus loved her and wanted her to give Him her heart so that He could live there. Grace rubbed a hand across her chest and felt the slight pounding beneath her sweatshirt. How did she go about giving Jesus her heart?

"Come all ye who are heavy laden, and I will give you rest."

Grace wasn't sure what that meant, but the man had said, "Come." She could do that.

She scrambled down to stand in front of her metal folding chair and looked up at her daddy. He was standing too - and frowning. Again. He seemed to do that a lot these days. His mouth was always pinched tight, and his eyes never laughed anymore.

She watched him grab her mommy's hand and gently pull the slight woman to her feet. Mommy was so different these days; a lot skinnier and always tired. When Daddy stood with her, she wobbled and her eyes rolled back in her head. Daddy had to catch her before she fell.

"Mommy?"

No answer.

Grace wasn't sure she knew this woman who was her mommy, yet wasn't. This woman who never did anything anymore, but sleep all day in the big hospital bed that was now in her parent's small bedroom.

Her daddy had to carry her mommy down the aisle because she couldn't seem to remember how to walk. Grace couldn't remember the last time she saw her walk. Grace followed right behind. Her hand gripped the back of her daddy's baggy jeans. She still wanted to give her heart to Jesus. Her daddy wanted the man up front to make her mommy all better. Grace did too.

She also wanted the gift that the man said she would get if she gave her heart to Jesus. But most of all, she wanted Jesus because He would never leave her. The man said that if she had Jesus in her heart, He would be with her always.

Her mommy was going to leave her soon. Grace didn't know how she knew this; she just did. She had watched her mommy get weaker day by day, and the fear of her leaving was a constant ache in the pit of her stomach. Grace desperately wanted the mommy back who played games with her and sang songs to her.

But Daddy had said that mommy was very sick and wasn't going to get better unless a miracle happened. And she had overheard Daddy tell Granma that he didn't believe in miracles anymore. Grace figured that meant mommy would be leaving her soon. If she had Jesus when her mommy left her, then maybe her heart wouldn't hurt so much.

At the end of the aisle, Grace stopped and watched as the man laid his hands on her mommy and listened as he muttered a prayer.

"Oh Lord, Jesus," the words suddenly boomed in Grace's ear and she stepped back, startled.

The man continued in the same booming voice, praying loudly, although she didn't understand all the big words. She rubbed her ringing ear and tuned him out; her thoughts flashed to the sermon.

"Just ask the Lord Jesus to be with you. Give him your heart and he will come to dwell with you. You will receive the gift of the Holy Spirit. A gift that will never be taken away from you. A magnificent gift. A gift so wonderful, it defies description. Don't you want to try it? Don't you want to receive this gift?"

Grace definitely did. She looked around her wondering what she was supposed to do next, but everyone was so busy, they seemed to have forgotten that she was standing there. A quick look showed people kneeling, some sitting, some clinging to one another and crying.

Grace followed the actions of an older man to her right and knelt. After listening to the man pray, she figured she could give Jesus her heart all by herself, just as easy as the next person could. She bowed her head and said her prayer out loud, just in case, just to make sure that Jesus heard it.

"Dear Jesus, that man over there said that if I give you my heart, I'd get a gift. But I've been thinking about it and you don't have to give me anything back. He said that you died for me, 'cause of all the bad stuff I've done. He said you know everything, so you know all that stuff I'm talking about. I'm sorry, I didn't mean to be bad, and I'm sorry you had to die for me. Help me to be a good girl." She paused, then, "Hey, I've got an idea! If you do give me a gift, let it be something that can help someone else. Like you did for me. That's all Jesus. You got my heart now. I reckon if you died for me and all you're asking for is that I do what you want, then that's okay by me. Amen, I guess. Um…bye. Oh, and if mommy leaves me, please don't let Daddy leave too."

Grace opened her eyes and looked up, anxious to share the fact that she now had Jesus in her heart. Her daddy had tears streaking his cheeks and her mother was very still, her face white, eyes shut. The preacher man didn't look so good either and people were backing away from the three of them.

Grace realized then that her mommy had left her. That bad word she kept hearing - cancer - had finally won and taken her mommy away. The feeling that someone had his arms wrapped around her made her look up. There wasn't anyone there. But then she remembered she had given Jesus her heart. That's where He was, in her heart, with his arms around her.

However that worked.

And she had her daddy. Sort of. He didn't have much time for her lately. But she had Jesus now.

Even though her mommy was gone now, she wasn't alone. Warmth flooded her and she rubbed the goose bumps that popped up on her arms. Somehow she knew that everything was going to be all right. She peeked up at her daddy.

He had his face buried in her mommy's hair and his shoulders were shaking. She linked an arm around his leg and leaned against him. His hand reached down to grab her and pull her close as though her presence gave him comfort.

Grace pulled away. Her daddy tried to pull her back, but Grace was determined. She resisted his tug, looked up into his sad eyes and pleaded, "Please Daddy, I need to hug her one more time, please."

A solitary tear dripped down his face to splash on her cheek. She brushed it away and felt him move; she realized her daddy wasn't holding her back anymore. He'd dropped to kneel on one knee, her mommy still clutched in his arms. Grace shifted closer and touched her mommy's face. It was warm and smooth and she finally looked like she wasn't in pain anymore.

Grace wrapped both her arms around the still form and squeezed as tight as she could. She laid her cheek on her mother's and whispered, "Bye Mommy, I love you. I have Jesus in my heart now. I'll see you in heaven. Tell Jesus I said hello."

A sob shook her daddy's shoulders so Grace transferred

her hug to his neck. He grabbed her with one arm and pulled her close; his other arm still clutched her mommy.

"It'll be okay, Daddy, I'll take care of you." Grace whispered as she brushed away the tears that slipped down his cheeks. And somehow, she firmly believed, Jesus would take care of them both.

Chapter 1

James Sinclair looked down at the thin, frail body of the fourteen-year-old boy lying listlessly in the queen-sized bed. He sighed and began to pace back and forth while he thought. How could this boy be his son? How? How could his son have this devastating illness?

Outside, thunder rolled and seconds later, lightening flashed, momentarily illuminating the room; rain lashed at the windows covered by the long, dark curtains. The one lamp on the bedside table gave off a soft glow.

The young, private nurse sitting in the recliner watched him with sorrow filled eyes. James ignored her, despising the pity she didn't bother to hide. If his son didn't need her, he'd get rid of her.

James rubbed his nose, and thought how he hated the smell of this room. Despite the fact that it was a spacious bedroom in a three-story mansion, it still smelled like a hospital room and that depressed him.

Weariness etched more lines in his already haggard features as he took the hand of the woman standing beside the bed, her fingers curled around the bed rail. She grasped his hand like a titanic survivor clutching a life raft. James rubbed her knuckles that had turned white with her grip. Her other hand held a tissue that had seen better days.

He spoke with quiet determination. "I'll find someone

who can help him. There's got to be someone in this vast world that can do something for him – in spite of what the doctors say."

Tears dripped off the woman's slightly pointed chin and the green eyes that lifted to his mirrored the hopelessness he felt, but hoped that he had well hidden from her desperate gaze.

A shaky hand dabbed the tissue across her face. "Oh James, he's dying. He'll be gone soon. His muscles are wasted; he's on oxygen, and sleeping all the time. How much longer can he last?" The last word ended on a high-pitched note that burned a hole in his heart.

"James? Pamela?"

He turned at the sound of his name. Geoffrey. His half-brother stood halfway inside the door as though unsure whether to venture further. The young man shoved his hands into his perfectly pleated khaki slacks; his shoulders hunched slightly.

The unconscious, nervous gesture surprised James as Geoff's confident, somewhat snobby attitude didn't leave room for nervousness. James ignored the uncharacteristic pose and said, "Come in Geoff. Come in." Despite their differences, he would always hold a fond spot in his heart for this man who was nine years his junior. "Come say hello to Seth."

Geoff stepped the rest of the way through the door, once again exuding confidence and self assurance. James decided he had probably imagined the brief attitude of nervousness.

Geoff made his way over to the other side of the bed. A well-manicured hand picked up the hand that was now skin and bones. James immediately noticed the contrast of strength and weakness. It almost made him retch. It wasn't fair that his son should have this horrid disease.

Seth's eyes flickered open for a moment and he tried to smile at his Uncle, but it was too much of an effort. His eyes closed and he drifted off again.

James heard Pamela choke back a soft sob.

"How much longer does he have?" Geoff's soft question speared James' heart.

"Not much," he spoke quietly just in case there was the slightest possibility of Seth being aware of the conversation in the room. "The doctors say there's nothing left to do, but keep him as comfortable as possible – unless we can find someone who can help him. As in a miracle."

"Does that someone exist?" Geoff asked skeptically.

"Yes. He – or she – has to. The Bible is full of healings. The blind, the lame, the deaf, the terminally ill. Why not now? In this day and age? I heard a preacher on television just yesterday claiming that the God written about in the Bible is the same God of yesterday, today and tomorrow. If that's true, he should still be in the healing business, right?"

"The Bible? Preacher?" Geoff's right brow arched in disbelief. "When did you start reading the Bible and listening to preachers?"

James glared at the younger man. "Since I've finally come to the realization; the…acceptance, if you will, that my son is going to die and the only thing left to save him is a miracle."

As James uttered the last word, his posture lost its defiance. Briefly, defeat and despair radiated from his being before he managed to gather himself together. He cleared his throat and threw his shoulders back. "I've got an idea, but I'm going to need your help, Geoff."

"My help?"

"What idea, James?"

Geoff and Pamela questioned him at the same time.

James looked back down at the wasted body and somehow managed to swallow the tearful lump that threatened to choke him. He reached out to brush the limp dark hair back from the unconscious boy's face. "I'm going to find us a miracle."

#

David Walton rubbed a hand across his eyes and stared at the marker. Lydia Marie Walton - Beloved Wife and Mother.

It had been two years. Two long years since Lydia had closed her eyes and drawn her last breath. He pulled the edges of his wool overcoat closer together to block out the worst of the wind. Fall had been their favorite time of year. Both had agreed that there was nothing like the smell of a cold, crisp day. A day like today. He breathed deeply, savoring the bite that nipped at his lungs.

David couldn't believe how much he still missed her. How much he longed to just hold her hand and sit down and talk with her. About anything and everything. Especially Grace. He couldn't help but smile when he thought about his precious six-and-a-half-going-on-sixteen year old.

He glanced up from his kneeling position to check on her. His darling, precocious child. David's eyes followed her as she chased a dry leaf dancing in the fall breeze. Blond curls cascaded in ringlets down her back and bounced lightly with each hopping motion she made.

The red wool hat barely kept the curls under control and from bouncing in her eyes. The cold weather sure didn't seem to bother her any. David shivered, but had to smile when a small hand swathed in a matching red mitten batted at the leaf. Her little girl giggles eased some of the pain that always seemed to stay centered in the vicinity of his heart.

"You'd be so proud of her, Lydia." David murmured the words in a soft whisper as he glanced back at the grave. He tugged of a glove and reached out a finger to trace the raised letters of her name on the marker. "She's so much like you - and so different. She changed when you died. She's quieter; feels things deeply, I think. She loves Jesus that's for sure. She's always talking to Him - or about Him. 'He's in my heart, Daddy. He's always with me and He'll never leave me, ya know.'" He quietly mimicked his sweet child, wondering if Lydia could hear him from heaven. Secretly, he envied Grace's wholehearted assurance that Jesus loved her.

What about me God? Have you forgotten me?

David dropped his head and felt a tear streak his cheek. He brushed it away, then tugged the glove back on his cold hand. "I need you, Babe. I need you more than God does. Grace needs you. I don't understand why He took you from us. Thanksgiving is just around the corner- four weeks from today – another holiday without you." He sucked in a deep, shuddering breath, then let it out slowly. "I'm trying not to be angry, but it's so hard. I wish I knew how to move on, to get back into life. Mom says I need to start dating again, that Grace needs a mother." A short, humorless laugh escaped him. "Can you imagine?"

David stopped his monologue and looked up to see Grace sitting on the ground beside a strange woman. He frowned. She had a small hand resting on the woman's upper arm and was talking earnestly.

David gave a small sigh and stood. "Well, Lydia, I've gotta go get our kid. She's talking to a stranger again. As quiet as she is most of the time, she picks the darndest times to become a regular motor mouth." He blew a kiss toward the direction of the grave, and then headed over to where his daughter and the woman sat.

He didn't try to disguise his approach, but neither did he announce his arrival. They either didn't hear him or they just ignored him. Grace didn't pause in her commentary and the woman never took her eyes from Grace's animated face.

"...so that's why we come here every Thursday afternoon. Daddy doesn't think Mommy can hear him anyplace but here. I try to tell him she's up in heaven and it doesn't matter where he talks to her, she'll hear him." Grace finally paused for a breath, so David popped in.

"Grace, what are you doing, honey?"

He watched her whirl to face him, innocence shining

brightly in her blue eyes. "Oh, hello, Daddy. I was just talking to the nice lady here. She's sad because her finance died, but she still likes to talk to him, so she comes here. She's just like you, Daddy. She thinks she has to come here to talk to him. I was just telling her that he could hear her from anywhere as long as he was in heaven."

David stared at his baby. This was the most he had heard her say in quite a while. She wasn't shy; she just never said a whole lot. She thought more than she spoke.

"Fiancé."

The soft voice brought his attention to the stranger.

"Huh?" He blinked. She was beautiful. Shiny red curls tumbled softly down her back. They looked almost exactly like Grace's only they were a beautiful, vibrant red instead of the white blond. The spattering of freckles on her nose and creamy cheeks fit her complexion by being cute, not overt. David blinked again when he found himself wanting to count them. Where did that feeling come from?

"Fiancé. Not finance." Her full lips were curved into a small, amused smile. The smile almost reached her green eyes. Almost.

He smiled back and held out a hand for Grace. As always, the feel of her small hand in his sent a rush of love so intense, he had to swallow twice before he could speak. "Grace often gets her words confused. Especially when she tries out new ones she's only heard once or twice. I hope she hasn't intruded."

"Not at all. I've enjoyed her company." David watched the woman shiver and realized that the sun was going down along with the temperature. She looked about as sturdy as that leaf Grace had been chasing just a short while ago.

Stepping closer to the woman, he held out a glove-encased hand. "David Walton."

Her smaller, bare hand gripped his larger one in a soft, yet strong clasp. There was more to her than he first thought.

A hidden strength. And she smelled like strawberries.

"Kristi Henderson." Her voice was smooth. It made him think of golden honey.

"Nice to meet you, but we've got to scoot. My mother always has supper ready and on the table at six sharp." He looked at his watch. It was ten 'til.

"Oh, well, it was nice to meet you too. Bye Grace." She wiggled her fingers at the little girl.

Grace giggled and imitated her motion. "Bye Miss Henderson."

Still holding Grace's hand, David turned and walked with a quick step toward the car, Grace skipping along beside him. It was getting colder; his mother was waiting; and the image of the beautiful stranger seemed to be permanently imprinted in his mind's eye.

David started the car and shook his head, hoping to return to his senses. He thought about Lydia. "Someday you'll meet someone." Her words had been a whisper a week before she died. "Give Grace a mother who'll love her as much as I do." David could tell that she had been trying to squeeze his hand. Her fingers merely twitched. He had lowered his cheek to hers and their tears had run together.

"Daddy."

Grace's voice jerked him back to the present. He looked over at her and saw her looking at him. Looking at him with those beautiful, compassion filled, blue eyes that knew too much; seemed to see things he couldn't see.

Could she really...?

He shut the question off before it formed in his mind. It didn't matter. It hadn't happened again.

"Yes, baby?" He reached out and tapped her little snub nose while offering her a smile through his pain.

"Mommy wouldn't want you to be sad. She's not. You can't be sad in heaven. She doesn't hurt anymore either."

David winced. "How did you know what I was thinking?"

Grace sighed, then gave him a smaller of version of the same smile Lydia used to flash at him when she humored him. "Well, it's kinda written all over your face. And, besides, you always look sad after we come here."

David's sigh echoed Grace's. "I know. And I know you're right too, about Mommy not being sad or in pain anymore. It's just hard being the one left here, you know?"

David felt Grace's eyes on him for a long moment before she spoke. Her next soft words were like a dagger through his heart.

"I know, Daddy. She left me too, remember?"

#

"Well?"

Dr. Kristi Henderson gripped the phone tighter and swallowed back her irritation. "Well what?"

"Did you see her?" The low voice didn't bother to suppress the thread of impatience woven through the short question.

"I saw her."

"And?"

"And what?" Kristi allowed her own impatience to be heard. She wasn't sure that what she was doing was the right thing and she didn't want give this man anything to work with until she was sure. "I saw her, okay? And I talked with her. She's a beautiful little six-year-old. She chased a leaf while her father visited her mother's grave." Kristi rolled her eyes wondering how she found herself in this situation. She was just trying to do her job – and find a way to get close to her sister. The one that wouldn't speak to her.

And this guy kept making it harder every day.

Kristi rubbed a hand down the side of her face. She was glad the person on the other end of the phone couldn't see the indecision she knew was stamped on her features. Was she doing the right thing? The question buzzed around her head like an irritating bee. Why was she so uneasy? This was MiracleCorp, the foundation that loved children, not hurt them.

"You promise not to...uh... hurt her, right?" Like she would even consider helping them if she really thought they would harm the little girl. Still, she wanted to hear him say it.

"Of course we're not going to hurt her," came the smooth – and slightly indignant - assurance. "We simply want to observe her - which is where you come in. We don't want to make a move or bring attention to ourselves if it's not necessary. Just find out about the child, then let us know one way or the other. Once you give us the information, we'll decide whether or not to pursue it."

Relieved at the answer, Kristi promised to call if she was able to gain any more information or another meeting with the little girl. Deep in thought, she lowered the handset of the cordless phone to the base.

Now what? What if she was wrong about Grace Walton? What if everything she heard was rumor? Grace certainly seemed like any other normal child. Talkative, inquisitive, carefree. And yet, she wasn't. She was different. Wise, compassionate, understanding. Not really like any other six year old she had ever met.

And those eyes. There was something about her eyes that seemed to see right into your very soul. Kristi shivered at the memory of those incredibly blue, blue eyes.

The first time Kristi had heard about the little girl was after church one beautiful Sunday morning about three months ago.

"Oh, Kristi, wait up!" Kristi had turned at the sound of her name to see Melinda Martin motioning for her to stop her descent down the front steps of the church. Kristi obliged with an inward sigh. The woman was sweet enough, but the word "leech" came to mind every time she set foot in the church and was forced to keep company with Melinda.

For some reason Melinda had taken a liking to her and attached herself immediately to Kristi's side whenever possible. At least the sun was shining and she wouldn't freeze if this turned into a long conversation.

Pasting a smile on her lips, she greeted the high-strung woman. "Hello Melinda, how are you this morning?"

"Oh, fine, thanks." Melinda brushed off Kristi's greeting with a wave of her perfectly manicured hand. Kristi raised an eyebrow, her curiosity piqued.

Melinda never brushed off a greeting – and she was never fine. She had a list of medical problems that she wanted everyone to know about and when she was done listing them, she thought her audience ought to respond in kind to her. Melinda wanted to know everything about everybody and if a body wasn't forthcoming with the appropriate amount of information, she usually responded with twenty questions. Not this morning. How odd.

Melinda rushed on. "I have something that I absolutely have to share with you," the woman gushed, grabbing Kristi's arm to pull her aside. Kristi followed simply because she couldn't pull away without seeming to be rude. Melinda's flawlessly made up face broke into a wide grin, but her voice dropped to a low whisper.

"I've got something for your work."

"My work?" This was the last thing that Kristi expected. Not many people knew what she did. Not that it was a secret, she just didn't advertise. She gently detached herself from the woman's grip with the pretense of brushing back the curls the slight breeze kept blowing across her eyes. She frowned in concentration. "Go ahead. What are you talking about?"

That was all the encouragement Melinda needed. "Well, you're just not going to believe what I saw this past Wednesday night."

Kristi gritted her teeth behind her smile. Was she going to have to drag it out of the woman? Instead, she stood silently, letting the expression on her face speak for her.

Melinda cleared her throat and continued. "Yes, anyway, I went to a healing service with my sister and her husband. Their daughter, Katie, my niece, has been diagnosed with an inoperable brain tumor."

Kristi gasped and immediately felt contrite. She reached out to touch the woman's arm. "Oh, I'm so sorry. I had no idea." She had been the one to suggest the child see a neurologist after hearing some of the symptoms from Melinda.

Being a doctor in a small church often came with a price. The price of free medical services and answering endless questions about numerous ailments. Kristi almost felt ashamed that she hadn't thought any more about the child since answering Melinda's questions several weeks ago.

Melinda's eyes fogged with tears for a brief moment, something so uncharacteristic of her usual bubbly self that Kristi had a small moment of insight into the woman standing before her. She wasn't all airhead.

Blinking the tears back, Melinda's expression cleared and she gave another one of her brilliant smiles. "But it's okay. She was healed that night!"

Kristi's brow shot up. "What do you mean - healed?"

"Healed. No more tumor. Not even a sign! The doctors can't believe it. They're calling her a walking miracle."

Kristi shook her head, feeling sorry for the poor woman. There had to be a purely scientific explanation. A faulty x-ray. A rare, but not unheard of, mix-up of patient information. Numerous explanations. Not that she believed that God couldn't perform a healing miracle in this day and age. She just wasn't sure that He did that anymore.

Being a doctor gave her plenty of opportunity to witness strange things. The human body was a strange thing in itself. A miracle really. Kristi smiled to herself even as she thought it. But to hear of a brain tumor just disappearing like that...well...

Melinda must have sensed her doubts for she pulled herself up and threw her shoulders back. "I saw it myself. That little girl just touched Katie on the head and prayed that Jesus would 'take away the bad thing growing in her brain'." The tears resurfaced. "And He did. I watched Katie's color come back. Her strength returned right there under that tent and she jumped out of her daddy's arms and started laughing. We haven't heard her laugh in months." Melinda gave a sniff and dabbed underneath her lower lashes to catch a lone tear before it fell on her perfectly powdered cheek.

"I just thought that since you work for MiracleCorp and all... I mean I know you're in the business of helping children while researching for medical miracles." Her voice trailed off and she gave a shrug, clearly deflated at Kristi's lack of enthusiasm.

Kristi mentally kicked herself. Since her sister had run away from home so many years ago, she had never intentionally hurt anyone again, but by allowing her skepticism to show, she had hurt this woman. "Well, I'm certainly glad that Katie is feeling so much better. God can do anything, that's for sure."

Melinda smiled, instantly appeased by the kind words. "Oh, she's definitely feeling better. The first thing she did when we got home that night was ride her bike around the block with her older brother, Michael. But Kristi, you wouldn't believe some of the things that I saw. That several of us saw. Katie wasn't the only one that little girl healed. Everyone she touched and prayed for walked out of that service changed and healed. God has something incredible in store for that child." The woman gave a small shrug. "Anyway, I just wanted to tell you since it sounded like something up your alley. I mean, you work at providing miracles to people and everything."

Kristi sighed. Some people just didn't get that the kind of miracles she dealt with didn't have anything to do with actual healings. It was just providing the medical expertise in order to make it possible for someone to live one last wish, or go on one last dream vacation – while researching for a cure for the disease that was killing them.

Melinda was still speaking. "Do with the information what you will. I only know what I saw that night. And I know what the x-rays show, or rather don't show anymore, on my niece's brain." She gave a little wave as she stepped back towards the thinning crowd outside the sanctuary of the church.

Kristi had watched Melinda turn away without another word. "Wait!" she had hurried after her without knowing why she had to ask. "What was the little girl's name? Did you catch it?"

"Grace. Grace Walton. I overheard her father say, 'Grace Walton, what in the world is going on?'"

Chapter 2

David rolled over and stretched an arm across the king-size bed. It was empty. Just as it had been for the past two years. When would he stop reaching for her?

Thanksgiving had come and gone. Somehow, the first week of December had crept up on him. Christmas was now on the horizon. Lydia used to go all out for Christmas; decorations everywhere, especially the mistletoe. David smiled at the memory. He could almost smell the cinnamon cider; taste the iced sugar cookies.

Lydia had been his high school sweetheart and they had gotten married the day after graduation. His eyes closed, he tried to bring up her image. It was getting harder to do it without first looking at her picture.

This time, instead of Lydia's pretty oval shaped face and blue eyes, a picture of flaming red curls, heart-shaped features and soft green eyes floated in his mind. David popped his eyes open, guilt stabbed his heart.

Oh, babe, I'm sorry.

David pulled the pillow over his head; berated himself a moment longer for his unfaithfulness, then stole a quick peek at the clock that was a foot from his nose. If he kept his eyes open, maybe he could get the woman out of his head.

He looked at the clock again and groaned out loud. The pillow landed at the foot of the dresser. He was going to be late. His appointment was across town in forty-five minutes. On a Saturday morning.

What on earth had possessed him to agree to a weekend meeting? His legs swung over the edge of the mattress, then stopped. His brain was finally waking up a little.

Wait a minute. Late? He frowned. His mother would never let him be late. As much as he hated to admit it, he relied on her more often than not.

His buddies often made fun of him; teasingly called him a "mama's boy." But it made her feel useful and David wasn't about to take that away from her. She often said that taking care of him and Grace kept her young.

Normally, she would make sure he was awake before putting on his required morning pot of coffee. Required because he was not a morning person. Pot of coffee because that's what it took to get him jump-started. David sniffed. No coffee.

Now he was worried.

Tugging on a pair of sweats that had spent the night on the floor next to his favorite gray sweatshirt, David stepped into the hall. It was awfully quiet. Disturbingly so. His mother never slept past 7:00. It was now 7:45.

His heart pounding, dreading what he would find, he slowly pushed open the door to his mother's room. Her frail form lay still under the blankets.

"Mom?" His voice was hushed. No answer. He forced himself to her side. "Mom!"

"Do you have to shout, boy?"

Her voice was barely a whisper, rasped out between dry cracked lips. Relief made his knees weak and he sank onto the bed beside her. When he picked up her hand, relief changed to worry. David could instantly feel the heat radiating from her. She was burning up.

"Mom, what's wrong? What hurts?" Even while the words were coming from his mouth, he was gathering her up in his arms, blankets and all. Flashes of Lydia's illness raced across his brain. All he could think about was that he had to get his mother to a doctor immediately. Her slight one hundred pounds felt like air as he carried her down the steps to the couch. He made sure she was settled then turned toward the stairs to go wake up Grace.

"It's just the flu, son. Could you get me some water?"

"Sure, Mom. I'll get you some water, then I'm going to get Grace and we'll get you to a doctor." He was halfway back up the steps when he did a u-turn back to the kitchen. Filling up a glass, he carried it to his mother, who barely had the strength to lift it to her lips. He helped her take a couple of sips, then set the glass on the end table.

"Be right back, Mom."

David took the stairs again, this time two at a time. He reached Grace's room, stepped inside and stopped to calm himself down before approaching her peacefully sleeping form and gently touching the little girl's shoulder.

"Grace. Wake up, sweetie." He gave her a small shake and watched her eyes pop open. Those blue eyes that never failed to make him look twice.

"Hi, Daddy." Her voice was rough with sleep. She gave a jaw-popping yawn and sat up. Two little fists rubbed away the rest of her sleep. David picked her up, cuddling her close and unconsciously inhaling her little girl scent.

"What are you doing? Where are we going?" She laid her head on his shoulder even as she questioned him; her innocent trust in him making his heart clench with a love that went beyond words.

"Granma's sick, hon. We need to take her to the doctor."

"Oh, okay." David started down the stairs with her. "Daddy, should I put some clothes on?"

He stopped and sighed. Right now, he wasn't having any trouble seeing Lydia's face. But it wasn't Lydia who was sick this time. It was his mother and it probably was just the flu. He had to get a grip.

"Yeah, put some clothes on, then come get in the car. I'm going to call the doctor and get Granma settled, okay?"

"Okay, Daddy. I wanna wear the pink shirt with the blue butterfly. Oh, you want me to pray for her?"

"No!" The word burst from his lips, harsh and biting before he could swallow it back.

Grace's lower lip trembled and her eyes filled with tears at his tone. She dropped her head to stare at the floor.

David took a deep breath and choked back fear and memories of two different nights filled with answers to prayers he didn't understand. The first one had been the night his wife had died. The last one was about six weeks ago.

Why he had gone to that healing service and taken Grace with him was a question he couldn't answer. David reached out a trembling hand to lift her chin and waited for her sad eyes to meet his. In a softer tone, he said, "No, Grace. As weird as it sounds, just…just…don't pray right now, okay?"

He hated to tell his child not to pray. It seemed wrong. It was wrong. But fear had a firm grip on him and he couldn't face what he knew about his only child. Not right now. If he kept ignoring it, it would go away. Wouldn't it?

"Okay, Daddy. I won't pray - right now. Will you tell me when I can?"

"Yeah. Yeah, of course I will." Tell her when she could pray? You're an idiot, Walton. What kind of father are you anyway? Lydia would know how to handle this. God, please tell me what to do. Are you even there any more?

# # #

"Here's the chart for the call-in, Dr. Henderson. They're on their way and should be here in about fifteen minutes. I know you like to get these in advance. The son is bringing in his mother. Thinks it's the flu."

Kristi looked up from her seat at the counter and smiled at the nurse. She reached out and took the proffered paperwork. Thank God she had a competent staff to work with. Without them, she would have been, if not lost, at least floundering. It had been a while since she had done this kind of doctoring. Actual diagnosing and working with human lives was a far cry from reading slides under a microscope. Kristi hadn't realized how much she had missed this.

She looked down at the chart in her hand and the smile slid off her lips. Name: Nancy Walton. Age: 80 years old. Walton. The right last name. The first name and age were all wrong. Kristi let out a frustrated sigh. She had been here for four weeks. It had been five weeks since she had met the father and daughter at the cemetery. Five weeks of dreaming about his sad blue eyes and heart stopping smile. Five weeks of telling herself she was building something out of nothing.

One week had been spent looking for Grace's doctor. It had taken Kristi so long to find the right one because she had started looking at Pediatricians first. Grace went to a family doctor. It figured.

Kristi was still uncomfortable with the method that she had used in order to find Grace's doctor. She had to act like she was treating Grace, but had lost the medical records that had been faxed to her. But if that's what it took to build their trust and gain an inside track to being able to communicate with her sister, then that's what she would do for now.

Her spiel of, "Hello, this is Dr. Kristi Henderson. I'm calling because we seem to have misplaced the records that were faxed to us. Could you please check the patient's chart to see when they were faxed and to what number? Her name is Grace Walton; age six years old. (She had given the age just in case there were two Grace Waltons out there.) Yes, I'll wait. Oh, you don't have a patient by that name? Well, I don't understand that. Let me check my records to make sure that I've got the right doctor's office."

And she would hang up and dial the next doctor in the phone book. She had finally hit pay dirt on her third day of calling.

Her boss had asked her to find the child so Kristi had brainstormed ideas about the easiest way to do that. Once she had found the right doctor's office, she had then approached her boss with the idea of working for the medical group in order to be able to see the child in a way that would allow her to be able to do certain tests and ask specific questions that wouldn't be thought of as out of the ordinary.

She had gained approval and gone immediately to work. One partner had quit without warning several months ago and the practice had yet to find a replacement.

Kristi gave God the credit for her open door. She firmly believed that He was orchestrating everything. She was just glad to be an instrument. Okay, God, what next? You got the grandmother here. What is it I'm supposed to do now?

Grace's grandmother. When Kristi had first arrived as the new doctor on staff, she had pulled the family's charts. David Walton - father. Nancy Walton - Paternal grandmother. Grace Walton - six-year-old daughter. Who never seems to get even the slightest cold.

Lately, Kristi had begun feeling rather uncomfortable with the work she was doing. This latest project seemed unethical and yet, technically, she wasn't doing anything wrong.

Except lying your way into an undercover job.

But cops did that all the time in order to help people, right? Still, she couldn't quite get rid of the nagging suspicion that all was not as it appeared to be. Kristi had come to work for MiracleCorp with the hopes of making a difference in the lives of hurting people – and with the hopes of reconciling with her sister.

Kristi finally decided she would continue doing what she could while trying to figure out a way to get to this child without her bosses knowing everything. They knew where she was, of course, and why she was there. After all, they had approved her plan.

But they didn't know when Grace came to the doctor. At least not as quick as Kristi would know it. And, Kristi hated to even admit it to herself, she wanted to see David again. Just to prove that the butterflies she had felt at their first meeting were completely due to finally meeting Grace face to face and nothing to do with Grace's drop dead gorgeous father. Yeah, right.

"Doctor?"

Kristi snapped her head around. Jenny, her nurse, was holding the door to the examining room open. The Waltons would have to wait. She had a colicky four week old and an exhausted mother to help. She really did love this part of her job.

#

David hated waiting rooms. They always smelled like cleaning solution that made his nose itch and his eyes water. And the crowd. They were always crowded and today was definitely no exception.

A young man with an ice pack on his hand. A couple of cases of the flu with hacking coughs that made David's throat hurt just listening to them. Sick children lying listlessly in their mother's laps. An elderly man with a hearing aid that kept squealing, talking much too loud and his wife writing notes in response. A wheelchair bound adolescent who looked angry at the world; legs twisted and useless.

David pinched the bridge of his nose and squeezed his eyes shut. The back of his head ached ferociously. Tension headache. Maybe he should tell them to pull his chart too.

He looked over at his mother who was seated across from him on one of the love seats. Her head rested against the back of the sofa, eyes closed. The unnatural flush to her cheeks told him she had a pretty high fever.

Grace sat beside him gently swinging her legs. "Daddy, can I pray now?" Her blue eyes still looked sad, like an overcast day.

"Yeah, why don't you pray all these people out of here so we can get done faster?" He didn't mean it sarcastically, he was just tired and worried. Having to cancel his appointment this morning didn't help either, although the client seemed to understand his dilemma. Family came first no matter the cost.

Grace got up and started walking around. Poor thing. She was going to be awfully bored if this turned into a long wait. He should have remembered to pick up a book for her.

She wandered over to admire a baby in a carrier.

"What's wrong with your baby?" David registered the words even as he continued his own train of thought. The baby let a horrible sounding cough that turned into a wheeze.

"She's got asthma. She needs a breathing treatment."

You would think they would take that baby on back. She sure didn't sound too good. David absently rubbed the back of his aching neck.

Grace lightly touched the infant on the head. "Grace," David reproved, "you shouldn't touch her."

Grace immediately pulled her hand back. "Sorry, Daddy."

The woman smiled at Grace. "That's all right. I hope she grows up to be as sweet as you are. Are you sick?"

"No, my Granma is. Daddy thinks she has the flu."

"Oh. That's tough. I'll pray that she gets better soon."

Grace's blue eyes lit up. "You love Jesus too?"

The woman let out a light laugh. "I sure do."

"Me too. I'll pray for your baby to get all better."

"Amber Jameson?"

The woman stood at the nurse's call and began gathering her things. "That's us. It was nice to meet you, Grace. I hope your Grandmother is feeling better soon."

Grace thanked her and waved good-bye. She moved on to the next person. David frowned. His daughter sure was turning into a little social butterfly lately. He gave a mental shrug and went back to his musings, thinking about the work to be done. He was in the process of making new cabinets for a very picky customer.

The young man directly to David's left, got up and walked around a bit, flexing his right hand. He then approached the window and told the woman behind it, "Cancel my appointment. My hand seems to be fine." He dropped the ice pack into the waist basket under the counter.

"Sir? Are you sure?"

"Yep. Thanks anyway."

David watched the fellow leave, still shaking his head and flexing his fingers.

A child pulled away from her mother's shoulder. "Mommy, I feel better. Can we go home now?"

The child jumped down and looked up at her mother. The feverish flush was gone from her cheeks, her eyes were bright and alert. The mother frowned and pressed a hand to the child's forehead. Confusion knit her brow.

"Hey, I feel better too." This from another child who all of a sudden looked perfectly healthy.

David sat up, beginning to take note of what was going on. His eyes flew Grace who was sitting next to the elderly man and woman who had been writing notes. Two more people requested a cancellation of their appointments and walked out the door.

David surged to his feet. He thought his heart was going to rupture right through his chest.

"Grace?"

"Yes, Daddy?" Her impish grin and sparkling eyes

alerted him instantly. She was doing this. His baby was doing this again.

"Stop it!" Fear was choking him. God, what are you doing to my child? Make it stop!

The elderly man reached up and yanked the hearing aid out of his ear. He gave it a shake. "Confounded thing is too loud."

"Too loud? You've never complained about that before." His wife was frowning.

"I know I haven't, but I am now." He was still shaking the hearing aid.

The woman gasped and grabbed his wrist. "Charles, you heard me!"

"Well of course...," his voice trailed off and his eyes widened in shock. He glanced down at the hearing aid in his hand, then back up to his teary-eyed wife. "I did, didn't I?" He looked around the waiting room. "I can hear every blasted thing in here!"

He gave a loud, "whoop" and clapped his hands.

David clutched Grace to him and looked into her innocent face. "Grace?" He swallowed hard. "Did you...?" He couldn't bring himself to ask the question.

"I didn't, God did." Grace answered his unasked question. "I just prayed for them to get all better." David closed his eyes and lowered his forehead to hers. "Oh Grace," he whispered.

"You told me I could pray so that we wouldn't have to wait so long. Can't I just pray for Granma now?"

David didn't know whether to laugh or cry. "Sure, honey. Pray for Granma now."

The door to the waiting room opened and several doctors walked in - including the redhead from the cemetery!

"What's going on in here?"

David read the nametag of the man who had spoken. Dr. Mitchels.

"Look Daddy! It's the lady from the cemetery. It's Miss Henderson." Grace was tugging on his hand. David was trying to swallow the lung that seemed to be lodged somewhere in his esophagus. She was definitely as beautiful as he remembered.

And she was coming his way. She got sidetracked when the young man in the wheelchair suddenly stood up. Kristi gasped and stumbled back, shock written all over her.

David subconsciously noticed the incredulous stares of the other two doctors, but his main focus was Kristi. She was staring open-mouthed at the young man who now towered over her. He was grinning, then he stomped his feet again and again. "I can feel 'em! I can walk!" His joyous shout echoed throughout the waiting room.

"Oh my God." David wasn't sure who the whisper came from, but it sure echoed his own prayer.

The touch of a hand on his arm brought his head around to see his mother standing next to him. In picture perfect health. "Mom?" His whispered question brought tears to her eyes. All she could do was nod.

"Let's get out of here." He reached around to grab for Grace, but didn't see her. Panic was close to setting in.

"Grace?" His shout brought Grace's attention to him. Along with everyone else's.

"Mr. Walton?"

There was that soft voice that he seemed to hear all the time now. He forced a smile, acting like he wasn't in the middle of the biggest miracle that had ever happened in this town.

"Dr. Henderson." She still looked a little shell-shocked, but was holding out a hand for him to shake. He grasped it without thinking. It was the softest thing he had touched in a long time. She was gazing over his shoulder at his mother.

"How are you feeling, Mrs. Walton?"

"Oh, I'm just fine now. Thank you. I was feeling a bit

poorly, but that seems to have passed. My son overreacts sometimes. It's because I'm old, you know, but I try to humor him." She gave Kristi a wink, who in turn forced a smile to lips that seemed to be made out of concrete.

The other doctors were fussing over the only patients left. The old man who could now hear and the young kid who could now walk.

"We're going to get out of here now. Let you doctors get things settled down." David was slowly nudging Grace and his mother toward the door.

"Wait!"

David ignored the plea and didn't look back as the door shut silently behind him.

During the short drive home, David's brain was clicking away, wondering what to do now? There was no way he could cover this one up. Someone was going to link those healings to Grace.

"Daddy?"

Grace's tremulous voice brought his gaze to the rearview mirror. Her blue eyes shimmered with tears just waiting to fall.

"What is it, sweetheart?"

"Are you mad at me? Did I do something wrong?"

David closed his eyes for a brief moment, then popped them back open to watch where he was going. "No, hon, you didn't do anything wrong and I'm not mad at you." How did he explain the situation to her? Would she understand? She was a smart child – and wise beyond her years, but the fact remained…she was still only six years old.

Before he could think of a way to explain it to her, the two men on his front porch caught his wary attention. Suits. Sunglasses. Stone-faced expressions. One thought flashed across his mind. Where's the TV crew? Was this a scene from a movie? Because those two guys standing on his porch fit the picture of government agents.

David put the car in park and climbed out trying for a nonchalance he didn't feel. "Can I help you fellows?"

The one on the left with the straight black hair cut into a bowl shape - David mentally dubbed him Moe - held out his right hand. "Hello, Mr. Walton. I'm Lyle Richards. This is my partner Mick Gentry. We've heard about your daughter and her rare gift of healing and we'd like to talk to you about possibly running some tests on her. We'd like to see if she could help other people." His expressionless black gaze shifted slightly. "Wouldn't you like that, honey?"

David turned to see Grace standing beside him. His mother was holding tightly to her small hand.

"Sure, I like to help people." Grace dimpled a grin up at the sober man. David felt his stomach acid start gnawing on his lining. He'd definitely have an ulcer soon.

"Uh, Mom, why don't you take Grace inside and see if she's hungry? I'll talk to these fellows out here." No way was he letting them in his house – or anywhere near Grace.

He crossed his arms across his chest and stared Moe in the eye. He couldn't think of him as Lyle. "Well, you don't waste any time getting right to the point do you? We just left the doctor's office ten minutes ago."

"We don't have time to waste, sir."

David noticed the man avoided the question of how they found him so fast. "I see. So, what's in this for Grace and me, should I decide to let you test her?" David wasn't interested in anything Moe and Curly could do for him. He was stalling, trying to read them and figure out how he could get them away from his little girl as fast as possible. How did they find Grace so quickly? Had they been watching her? David broke into a cold sweat just thinking about it.

Moe and Curly glanced at each other and smirked. David knew what they were thinking. Anyone can be bought. "Well, sir, we just happen to have one hundred thousand dollars with your name on it. All you have to do is bring Grace to MiracleCorp headquarters first thing in the morning."

"One hundred..." David really was in shock. He had no idea they would just offer him that kind of money standing on his sidewalk. He swallowed and tried to play it cool. "Uh, well, that's hard to resist. One hundred thousand, huh?"

Another glance between the two men made David feel like scum. What if he told them they could take their money and shove it? How far would they go to get Grace? Acting like he would even consider the offer left a bad taste in his mouth. But something told him to play along.

"So, do I get half up front?"

# # #

The two men walked to the black sedan on parked on the curb. Mick opened the door passenger door and turned to his partner who was making his way to the driver's side. "Do you think he's really going to bring her?"

"Nope, I think he's playing us. He was scared spitless."

"So, why didn't we just pop him and grab the brat?"

"Because, you idiot, the boss said to keep a low profile. He don't want anything bad coming down on the foundation. He's got a reputation, remember? And besides, we kill her dad, that kid ain't gonna do nothin' but cry. We might need him to get her to cooperate with us."

"True, so what're we gonna do? Just sit back and let him figure out a plan how to keep us from getting' our hands on the girl?"

Lyle slammed the door and shoved the key in the engine. "Of course not. Doncha know that the boogey man comes out at night?"

"Yeah, right. The boogeyman. Guess that'd be us, huh?"

"You're brilliant, Mick, absolutely brilliant."

Chapter 3

Kristi flipped on the six-o'clock news and settled back in the recliner to finish her TV dinner of stiff Salisbury steak and even stiffer mashed potatoes. She gave a grimace and shoved the meal away.

When a camera panned the doctor's office where she had just finished her unusual day's work, Kristi scrambled for the remote to turn up the volume. Where was it? She couldn't find it fast enough, so she just turned it up manually.

"Today, in this very doctor's office, Eastgate Family Practice, a group of Christian doctors, saw a miracle happen."

A miracle? Ha, more like miracles.

The reporter, a striking young woman in her mid thirties, turned to look at the building behind her.

"We are filming live, trying to catch someone who witnessed these incredible events."

It wouldn't be long now. Dr. "What's-his-face" is going to be the spokesman and milk this one for all it's worth.

Even as the thought flashed across her brain, the handsome young doctor Kristi had been thinking about stepped out the front door. He flashed his perfect toothpaste ad smile and stepped toward the reporter.

"Doctor, could you give us an idea of what happened here today? The word has spread like wildfire. Tell us about these miracles we've heard so much about."

When she shoved the microphone under his chin, the flashing smile never slipped. "Well, they occurred around 9:00 this morning. We open at 8:00 and just an hour later, people were canceling their appointments saying they were healed."

The reporter brought the microphone back to her mouth. "We have a short clip caught just moments earlier of a young mother and a baby."

The scene began with the same reporter talking to a woman who appeared to be in her mid-twenties.

"...has asthma. She seemed to be having more problems than usual breathing this morning so I brought her in first thing. By the time I was called back to the examining room, she was sleeping peacefully and hasn't had a problem since."

"Do you know what happened? How did her healing take place?"

"I honestly don't know. She was sick one minute and fine the next." The mother gave a small shrug, then smiled slightly. "The only thing I can think of is that a little girl's prayers worked a miracle."

"Little girl?"

The woman flushed, and looked down for a moment. "Well, all I know is that a little girl in the waiting room said she would pray for my baby. Now she's fine. It just goes to show you the power of God, and the fact that He's always listening."

"Uh, yeah. Power of God. Well," the reporter seemed at a loss for words for a short moment, "that's it for WJKA news reporting live. We'll return with more the moment we have an update for you."

Kristi finally located the remote. It was wedged between the cushion and the edge of the recliner. She pressed the power button to shut the TV off and sat in the silence of her home. *All I know is that a little girl in the waiting room said she would pray for my baby. Now she's fine.* Kristi rubbed the chill bumps that stood out on her arms.

Could it be possible? Could that little girl really pray people back to health? She immediately flashed to the young man who had almost knocked her down when he jumped out of his wheel chair.

It had to be the little girl. There was no other explanation.

Just thinking about the ramifications made Kristi's brain hurt. When she first started out on this quest, she hadn't given enough thought to what she would do if she actually found the girl.

"Find the girl," they had ordered her. "Find her and see if she's legit. Then bring her to us."

Kristi pulled her bible from the end table. God, only you know what's really going on. Show me what to do with the information I've got.

Her bible fell open to 1 Samuel 27:1 "But David thought to himself, 'Saul will catch me someday. The best thing I can do is escape to the land of the Philistines. The he will give up looking for me in Israel, and I can get away from him.'" (New Century Version - The Everyday Bible)

What does that mean, Lord?

Kristi flipped forward to Proverbs. Her heart beat faster as she read the scripture God laid before her. Verse 10. "My child, if sinners try to lead you into sin, do not follow them." Her eyes skipped down the passage to verse 15. "My child, do not go along with them; do not do what they do. They are eager to do evil and are quick to kill." And verse 18-19. "But sinners will fall into their own traps; they will only catch themselves! All greedy people end up this way; greed kills selfish people."

The Lord was speaking right to her. Kristi knew it. She also knew that something big was getting ready to happen and she needed to be ready when it did.

The jarring ring of the phone jerked her from a slight doze. She glanced at the clock. 11:03. Exhaustion had won and she had slept for about four hours.

"Hello."

"Kristi!" The voice was breathless, scared.

"Tess? What's wrong?" She gripped the handset tight.

"Kristi, you've got to get in touch with David and his little girl. You've got to get them somewhere safe. Something's going on. They're not happy with that newscast tonight. And the fact that you didn't tell them about Grace and what went on in the doctor's office." Tess's voice was a mere whisper. "They're going to his home tonight to kill him and kidnap Grace. Then they're going to report that Grace died so they can do whatever they want to with her without any interference. They're crazy! It's supposed to look like a random murder/robbery kind of thing."

"Tess, are you sure? How do you know this?"

"I just know! I was working late on some stuff and overheard half of a phone conversation. I don't know who the man was; never seen him around here before. I was in a part of the building I don't normally go to, but when I passed by an office, I heard the name Walton and listened in. Thank goodness whoever he was had his back to the door or I'm not sure I would be able to tell you this information. Now get them away, somewhere safe…fast!"

The phone clicked. Kristi realized she was shaking.

"Oh, God, help me know what to do."

The best thing I can do is escape…

The words she had just read from 1 Samuel whispered across her mind. And suddenly she knew what she had to do. Kristi grabbed the cordless handset and punched in David Walton's phone number.

#

David heard the phone ring and immediately rolled to the right to grab the thing from the nightstand. He fumbled it, caught it and barked into it. " 'Lo?"

"Mr. Walton?"

"Yeah?"

"Mr. Walton! Wake up. This is an emergency!"

His sleep-fogged brain went on full alert. "What? Who is this? What's the emergency?"

"You need to get Grace and your mother and get out. They're on their way to kill you and grab your daughter. I'll explain everything later. Right now, just please trust me!" David could hear an almost desperate fear for him coming through the phone. It made the hair on his neck stand up. Who in the world...? Her fear fueled his, bringing up visions of the two goons who had greeted him on his doorstep only hours before.

"Right. Okay, where should I go? Won't they know my car?"

"Meet me by the water fountain at Bartlett Park in fifteen minutes. Hopefully by the time they find your car, you'll be long gone. I'm in a black SUV."

David didn't bother with goodbye - or asking her name again. The fear in her voice was enough to motivate him to action – along with the vivid memory of the earlier visit by the two men in black. Throwing back the covers, he threw some clothes into a suitcase, then raced into his mother's room to shake her awake.

"Mom, get dressed and pack a bag. Hurry! We're all in danger and we've got to get out of here now. I'm going to get Grace. Meet me in the car."

"What? David? What's going on, son?"

"I'll explain later. Now hurry, please!"

He was grateful she didn't ask any more question, and as soon as he saw she had a suitcase open and was tossing some things in it, he raced down the hall to Grace's room.

His precious child, so innocent and unaware of the magnitude of her gift. God, why her?

He grabbed her backpack out of her closet and threw in some jeans and sweatshirts. A favorite toy and a couple of videos and her toothbrush followed.

"Daddy?" Apparently he hadn't been very quiet while packing.

"Hey, sweetie, we're going on a little trip for a while. Come on and get in the car."

"But it's dark outside." Small fists rubbed at her eyes and she laid her head back on her pillow.

"Get up, baby. I know you're still sleepy, but you can sleep in the car, okay?"

She groaned and pulled the covers up over her head.

"Grace, get up now!" he yelled. He watched her pop up from under the covers. Wide-awake blue eyes registered shock. David never yelled at her.

He lowered his voice and grappled with his fear. "Come on. I'm sorry I yelled, but this is really important, okay?"

Grace nodded. "Okay, Daddy." She raced down the stairs without another word. David was right behind her.

#

Kristi's fingers tapped the steering wheel; her gaze anxiously watching the street. Would David make it before those goons got to his house? A fervent prayer on her lips, she made a conscious effort to slow her breathing. Be anxious about nothing... Kristi repeated the verse over and over, hoping it would take root in her anxious heart.

He should be here by now. Had they found them? Had her phone call been too late? Jesus, please...

Pleading turned to thankfulness when she saw his car turn the corner and head toward her. Oh, thank you, thank you...

Kristi rolled her window down. David did the same. "We have to ditch your car somewhere."

"You!" His voice shook with anger and recognition. "What is this? A set up? You people are not getting your hands on my daughter!"

"No! Wait!"

But anger mixed with worry and fear for his child was not a combination that incited listening. Kristi watched him peel away from the curb, tires squealing. Another look down the street brought her heart in her throat. A black sedan came into view.

Oh dear, Lord...

Kristi wheeled in behind David's red Explorer. She'd just follow him. He'd have to stop eventually. Maybe once he'd cooled off he'd listen to reason. But first, she had to make sure they lost the guys behind them.

A quick glance in her rear view mirror only reflected darkness. Had they not seen them? Kristi frowned and wondered if that were possible.

Then it hit her. The sedan had been going in the direction of David's house! Relief swept over her. They hadn't even been to his house yet. That gave her a little more time to catch up to David and convince him that she was on his side and that he needed her help to keep his family safe.

She just had to figure out how to tell him that his family was in danger because of her. But that could come later.

Much later.

Chapter 4

James leaned back in his luxurious leather chair and gazed out the window. The plush office was located on the twenty-second floor of the MiracleCorp building located in downtown Greensburg, South Carolina. However, his eyes never focused on the beautiful skyline glowing in the dark night.

It was pitch black outside right now, but tomorrow, the sun would be shining, people would be laughing, and his son would still be dying. How could the world not stop? How could God allow this to happen? After everything he had done for this city - for this country?

The sigh came from the soles of his alligator shod feet. When his door opened, he didn't bother turning around. Expensive cologne drifted his way. His brother had expensive tastes also. Probably the only thing the two men had in common. No, they had one other thing, but James pushed that thought out of his mind. "Did you find her?"

"Yes...and no."

In an angry motion, James swiveled the chair fast to face Geoff. "And what exactly does that answer mean?" His tone was hard; his face granite.

"Exactly what I said. We found her, paid the dad off, went to get her – and they ran." One shoulder lifted in a shrug. The motion made James' blood pressure rise several notches.

"And?" The word was ground out between clenched teeth.

"We're on it. Don't worry, we'll find her."

James stood and circled the desk to stand in front of Geoff. The hostility in the young man's eyes caused him to realize that he needed to gain control. Alienating him wasn't going to do either of them any good. He paused, then leaned back against the solid mahogany desk and crossed his arms. "Okay. You found her. Mr. Walton took the money and ran. What sent him running?"

Another lackadaisical shrug. "Who knows?"

James let his shoulders sag. "Geoff, my son is getting worse by the day." He barked out a short humorless laugh. "No, he's getting worse by the hour. I need this little girl. She's Seth's last chance and I don't care what it takes to get her. Do you understand me?"

"I understand you clearly, James, but there's only so much I can do. I've got the fellows on it."

James walked back around to his chair and sank into it. "Yeah. Okay. Keep me posted, right?"

"Of course. What I know, you know."

Geoff headed for the door.

"Hey Geoff."

His hand on the knob, he turned back to look at James. "Yeah?"

James offered up a weary smile that conveyed a silent apology. "Thanks."

Geoff's defensive posture eased somewhat, he even offered a small smile in return. "Sure. He's my nephew, right?"

"Right. Hey, I hear you're dating someone." Changing the subject always helped when it got to be too much to think about anymore.

The young man looked startled for a moment before a shy smile drew the corners of his lips up.

"Yeah. Yeah, I am."

James cleared his throat. "Well, uh, that's good, right?"

"I sure hope so, James, I sure hope so. She's definitely not like anyone I've met lately. She intrigues me - and she's very helpful. Always doing something for someone." Another small smile. "You'd better get home. Pamela needs you."

James never heard the door click. He was too busy staring back out the window pondering his son's short future ...and praying – in his own way – for a miracle.

#

Geoff headed back to his office. As head lab "rat," he shouldered the responsibility of overseeing all testing done in MiracleCorp's extensive, state of the art laboratory. He was proud of his position; enjoyed the power that came with it. He spoke and people jumped as fast for him as they did for his brother, James.

James. The man was starting to annoy him. Treating him like he was nobody. Ordering him around. Find the girl, James told him. Bring her to me. Who did James think he was, anyway?

Geoff snorted. James had always beaten him at everything. Sports, business...love. Geoff shut off that train of thought and focused back on the search for Grace. Well, where was she anyway? How could she have disappeared like that? Why had the father picked her up and run? What had scared him?

Geoff decided why they had run didn't matter right now, rather where had they run was the most important question. He shook his head and picked up the phone. He would find out if the Walton's had any family that they could run to. He would send the guys out to do a sweep of those family members without letting them know they were being watched. If they spotted the girl, they could pick their opportunity and snatch her.

Geoff had told James he would do his best to find the child. He would keep searching and he would find her. James could count on him for that.

#

David's fist hit the steering wheel; frustration oozed from every pore. A drop of sweat slid from his brow to tickle the end of his nose. He lifted his left shoulder to brush it on his shirt.

"What's going on Daddy?"

The fear in his daughter's voice echoed the fear in his gut. Desperate to keep her from knowing how scared he really was, David cut the car sharply to the right, then slowed down. Where he was going, he had no idea. He just knew that he had to get somewhere safe. Lights flashed out at him from the businesses lining the empty streets. "We're taking a little trip, honey. Just try to sit back and relax, okay?"

"Okay." The soft word was uncertain, but she trusted her Daddy. David hoped he could live up to that trust.

The ringing of his cell phone startled him so bad he almost ran off the road. What in the world? Who...? He snatched it from the cup holder and slapped it to his ear.

"Hello," he barked.

"David, don't hang up!"

"Who is this?"

"This is Kristi Henderson. The woman you ran from a few minutes ago. I'm right behind you and we need to talk. Now."

"Lady, you are out of your ever loving mind!" David was so angry he couldn't think straight. And if he ever needed to think straight in his life it was now.

He hung up.

What should he do? His mind clicked furiously coming up with possibilities and discarding each one. Right now, he needed some cash – untraceable cash - and a cheap hotel room.

"David?"

His mother's voice reminded him all over again the responsibility now resting on his shoulders. His family was in danger and it was up to him to keep them safe. A glance in his rearview mirror told him that Kristi was still behind him.

Before he could answer his mother, his cell phone rang once more. He looked at the number. It was her again. He didn't bother with a greeting this time.

"Look, I don't know how you fit into all of this, but ever since we've met, I've had nothing but trouble, now stay away from us!"

"Wait!" Her shout made him pause, the desperation in her voice finally making its way through the fear fogging his brain. She pleaded, "Just listen to me, please. You've got to listen or you're going to end up dead!"

Okay, she had his attention. Definitely not his trust, but she did have his attention.

"How do you know everything you know? And how did you get this number?"

"I have friends in high places, but we can go into that later. Right now, you need to get you and your family safe."

"My thoughts exactly. Any suggestions?" Not that he would take them.

"Yes." The relief in her voice was obvious. "Drive out of state. Get on I-26 and go toward Asheville, North Carolina. Find a hotel and check in. Do you have any cash? Don't use your credit cards."

"Oh, yeah. I've got cash." David glanced at the suitcase on the floorboard of the passenger side. "I just don't know if

I want to use it. It could be marked or something."

"What?"

"Yeah, they paid me to turn my daughter over to them. I took the money to buy some time, then I got your phone call and here we are. I need to do something with this money before they call the cops on me. And why I'm telling you all this I don't know." David practically growled his frustration into the phone.

"Would you be willing to stop and meet with me?"

"Who are you?"

"Just someone trying to make sure that I'm listening to what God is leading me to do."

God.

David ran out of steam. "Fine. You lead."

He had nowhere to go, no idea who he was running from, or who to trust. He had to start somewhere; he might as well start with someone who was trying to follow God. At least He knew what this was all about.

# # #

Kristi gripped the wheel, pressed the gas pedal to the floor and zoomed around David to take the lead. Thank you, God for making him listen to me. Please tell me what to tell him so that he'll trust me and keep listening to me. And keep Tess safe.

The prayer whispered from her lips. She continued to pray for guidance and wisdom as she drove west on I-26, then I-40. Soon signs for North Carolina and Asheville zipped past her window. She was doing exactly the speed limit as she had no intention of being stopped. David still followed silently behind her.

Kristi soon realized that getting a hotel this time of the year was going to be no easy thing. Biltmore House was the main attraction right now. People flocked to see the mansion so elaborately decorated and open to the public. "No vacancy" signs were prominent on the billboards of the hotels located along the interstate.

It was end of prime tourist season as far as the foliage was concerned. Kristi could envision the beautiful orange, brown and gold colors of the leaves that were only just beginning to die. People came from all over the country to enjoy the scenery to the very end.

Punching in David's cell number once again, she waited. It rang once.

"Hello."

"Mr. Walton...," she began.

David interrupted. "Just call me David. Where are we going?"

Kristi sighed. "I hate to say it, but I wish I knew. I don't know where we'll be able to find a hotel with a vacancy at this time of the year."

David's sigh echoed hers. "What about a bed and breakfast? It's almost one o'clock in the morning. I've got to get mom and Grace in a bed."

Kristi perked up. "A bed and breakfast? That's an idea, although they're probably full too. But, we've got to start somewhere. I'm going to look for a gas station so I can check out a phone book."

"Great." His tone was flat; weary. Kristi's heart went out to him and a flash of guilt darted through her. Oh, how she wished she had done some more research and thinking before leading MiracleCorp to this little family. She bit her lip. Please God, protect them - protect us. And find a safe place for us to stay for the rest of the night.

Kristi spotted a gas station and wheeled her black Suburban into the parking lot. She pulled up to the pay phone and climbed out. The smell of smoke from a nearby fireplace greeted her along with a blast of cold wind. A quick tug pulled her coat tighter against the back of her neck. David parked beside her, but left his Explorer running.

Kristi noted the bright red color of the car. He was going to have to ditch it somewhere. Her "friends" probably had put an APB out on it the minute they realized the Walton's weren't at home.

She grabbed the phone book that was hanging by the cord and flipped it open to the yellow pages. She found the listings for the local B & B's.

"Whatcha got?" David's breath shivered across her ear and made her jump. He was tall, head and shoulders taller than her. He had his hands in the front pockets of his jeans and his shoulders hunched against the elements. No jacket, of course.

Kristi cleared her throat. "How about this one?"

"I really don't care as long as it has a bed. Just start at the top and start calling until you find one." Impatience resonated in his voice.

Kristi slammed the phone book shut and turn swiftly to jab a finger in his chest. His wince gave her immense satisfaction. She'd had enough. "Now look here. I'm sorry you've found yourself in this unholy mess and I know you're worried sick, but you can take your nastiness and keep it to yourself. I'm just here to help you, but if you want to do this on your own, then I'm out of here."

David was rubbing the spot on his chest and looking contrite by the end of her tirade.

"Well, well, well. A temper to match the hair." His blue eyes twinkled and his hand reached out to rub a silky red strand between his fingers.

Kristi swallowed hard. That was the last kind of response she had expected to her outburst. It was a rare moment of an intense kind of connection as his blue eyes held her green ones.

"Daddy? I need to use the bathroom." And the moment was gone; interrupted by a sleepy child.

David blinked, reality crashed back in, and his eyes were once again cloaked with sorrow and worry. Kristi mourned the loss, but turned back to the pay phone while David attended his child.

It took six calls and twenty minutes, but Kristi finally managed to wake the innkeeper of The Mountain Home Bed and Breakfast in Mountain Home, North Carolina. David had managed to find some scratch paper and a pen for Kristi to scribble down the directions. She hung up and rubbed her left ear, sore from pressing the receiver against it.

"Here we go." She waved the paper at him. He had come up behind her after putting Grace back into the car. "Climb in and follow me. It's off of Exit 13. We'll have to back track a little bit, but I think that might be a good thing. Who would guess we'd be staying in this obscure little town?"

"We're right behind you." David climbed in the Explorer and shut the door.

#

David followed Kristi back down the interstate to Exit 13. Fatigue made the journey seem much longer than the actual ten minutes it took, but finally they pulled up beside a discreet stone house nestled high on a hill. The front porch light said they were expected. Smoke gracefully rose in a thin stream from the stone chimney, weaving its way upward to disappear into the night.

David hoped that he and his small family could disappear just as easy. He gave the home the once over and thought it rather non-descript, but then decided that was probably a good thing. In fact, as long as it had a comfortable bed, he didn't care what it looked like. He parked next to Kristi and waited as she approached his side of the car. David opened the door and stepped out.

"We're upstairs." Kristi's voice was soft, hushed in the

dark, cold night. "The innkeeper said he'd meet us over here. He and his family live next door. When we open the front door, he will hear some kind of chime that will let him know we're here."

David shook his mother awake, then gathered a sleeping Grace into his arms. Her familiar little girl scent made him clutch her close. He was beginning to wish he still prayed so he could pray for her safety.

He'd get them settled then come back for the three small suitcases. Kristi already had the front door open when David walked up onto the porch. His mother followed close behind, keeping her hand against his back to help her balance.

"Hi there. I'm coming. Be there in a second. Go on inside and make yourself comfortable," a voice called from the shadows. A transplant from somewhere up North, David thought.

"No problem," he answered.

They weary foursome made their inside. The interior was much fancier than the exterior led one to believe. The front door opened directly into the living room. The small fire in the fireplace gave off a cozy glow. It was slowly dying to become glowing embers.

David's mother lowered herself into an antique armchair. Kristi slumped on the beautiful 1800's couch and David merely stood to the side of the doorway, Grace peacefully snoring against his shoulder, his coat tucked snuggly around her. He softly blew away a blond curl that was tickling his nose. The door opened once again and David shivered at the gust of cold air that blew through.

"Okay folks, here we are. I'm Mike. If one of you will just sign your name in the book, I'll show you upstairs. You really lucked out tonight." He gave a hearty chuckle that grated on David's already sprung nerves.

"Or I lucked out, depending on how you look at it. Got a call around 11:00 from the family that was supposed to stay here tonight. Whole family came down with the flu. Thought I was going to miss out on a lot of money. Then you guys called. Great timing."

Mike flashed them a smile and continued his dialogue as he proceeded up the steps. "Got two queen beds and a pull out sofa. Linens and everything are already set out. You're good to go. Feel free to yell if you need anything else. Oh, yeah, seeing how late it is, you guys probably want to sleep in in the morning, so we'll leave you some breakfast in the fridge on the middle floor. Just help yourself and pop it in the microwave. If you need anything, let me know. My little girl's got the chicken pox, so I'll probably be up all night anyway."

David entered the room nearest the doorway and gently tucked Grace into one of the queen beds while Kristi thanked the man and saw him out the door. David stepped back out of the room to add his thanks when he felt Grace standing beside him. Her sleepy voice stopped Mike's exit. "Your little girl's sick?"

"Yeah, she's got itchy bumps all over her poor little body, so she's pretty miserable."

David gave a soft warning. "Grace, it's time for you to go to sleep."

Blue eyes stared up at him, unblinking and definitely wide awake now. "But Daddy, I need to go see her."

"No." David bit out the word, harsh and hard.

Grace flinched and tears pooled in her eyes. She whispered, "Please?"

Mike's rough voice interrupted the father/daughter conflict. "Uh, is everything okay?"

David forced a smile through stiff lips. "Sure, we're great. And very appreciative of you letting us in so late."

Mike slapped a hand on David's back in friendly camaraderie. "Sure, no problem."

Grace piped in softly, "I'll pray for your little girl.

What's her name?"

"Sylvia. Her name's Sylvia. She's three years old."

"Okay," Grace beamed a sweet smile at the man. "I'll pray that God heals her tonight."

"That's enough, Grace!"

"David..." He felt his mother's calming hand on his arm.

Mike spoke up. "Well, thank you, little girl, I sure would appreciate that. She's just been miserable with the bumps itching and the fever, so if you think your prayers will help her, you go right ahead."

"'Kay, Mr. Mike. Nite."

"Good night, folks. Get some rest."

David watched Kristi usher the man out, then turned back to Grace. "Grace, you've got to stop this."

"Why Daddy? Don't you want me to listen to God?"

What the heck was he supposed to say to that? "Just stop, okay?"

"But can I pray for her?" Grace persisted.

David pondered the question. It wasn't like the little girl was in the room with them. And all the other people Grace had healed, she had actually touched. So maybe if she wasn't in the room...."Sure Grace, you go ahead and pray for her."

"Thanks Daddy." A peaceful curved her lips and she slipped beneath the covers again.

His mother made her way to the bathroom and David pulled out the sleeper sofa. Kristi stepped up to the other side of the bed and took one end of the sheet to help him make it up.

"I'll take the sofa," she said softly. "You can have the other bed and your mother can sleep with Grace."

David shrugged. "Thanks, but I don't mind the sofa. You take the bed."

Kristi gave a small laugh. "Are we going to argue about this the rest of the night?"

"Probably, we've argued about everything else so far."

David flashed her a weary grin.

Kristi grinned back at him. "Are we agreeing on that?"

He felt his knees wobble a bit. What's up with that? Just because she's got a great smile and is a beautiful woman doesn't mean you have to get all weak-kneed, Walton, David scolded himself and barked a small laugh. "Yeah, I guess so. That's a first, huh?"

He cleared his throat and looked at the bed. "You know it doesn't matter where I sleep. I'm going to conk out and not know anything until morning anyway." At least he hoped he would. Right now, he felt pretty confidant that whoever was chasing them wouldn't find them tonight. And if they did, he hoped that they wouldn't try anything with a house full of people.

"Then take the bed," Kristi ordered.

Too tired to argue anymore, David nodded. Ignoring her small victory grin, he headed for the car to retrieve the suitcases. Standing beside his Explorer, David noticed that the drive curved down behind the house, effectively hiding their vehicles from the road.

The fear clutching his chest eased off somewhat allowing him the first deep breath he'd taken in hours. He grabbed the cases from the back and headed back into the warmth of the house.

Upstairs, he made use of the bathroom, then wandered into the other room to check on Grace and his mother. His mother's back was to him, but she didn't stir.

Grace lay on her back; arms thrown above her head. Her fingers curled into loose fists, she slept peacefully, blond ringlets spread in wild abandon over the pillow. A light flush on her cheeks; she slept the sleep of the innocent.

David reached down to touch one of the curls. It grasped his finger and wrapped itself around the digit like it had a will of its own. He ran a thumb over the silky strands, then leaned down to place a soft kiss on his daughter's forehead.

He whispered, "Sleep tight, baby, don't let the bed bugs bite. Daddy loves you to pieces."

David returned to the other room then climbed between the sheets. He stared at the ceiling for a brief moment wishing he could pray. However, the words wouldn't come, so he let Kristi's quiet movements in the small room next to him lull him to sleep; her pretty green eyes laughing into his was his last mental picture before sheer exhaustion overtook him.

Chapter 5

An annoying, consistent chirping brought Kristi's head out from under the downy soft pillow. She cast a bleary eye toward the window and frowned at the little blue bird sitting on the ledge. If she didn't know better, she'd swear it was trying to wake her up on purpose.

"Go 'way," she whispered. "It's too cold to be outside. Go fly to Florida or something." The bird gave one last chirp and flew away. Kristi blinked, then shook her head. A quick glance around at her surroundings and the bird was forgotten. The night before was not.

She eased out from under the sheet and walked to the window. She glanced outside, wondering if they were safe - or if someone was waiting outside ready to pounce the minute they walked out the front door.

Kristi shivered and walked back the backpack she had hastily packed the night before. She grabbed a sweatshirt and pulled it over her head. Crossing the small den, she tiptoed over to peek into the bedroom where Grace and David's mother were still sleeping soundly.

She then padded silently to the other bedroom. The door had been left slightly ajar - no doubt in case Grace woke in the middle of the night and needed her daddy. David was buried under pillows and the down comforter. His quiet snores made her grin. She had the time she needed for her daily quiet time.

Kristi crossed back to the small den area and rummaged again through the pack. She easily found what she was searching for.

Her Bible.

It was 8:30, much later than she normally woke, but she decided to carry on with her quiet time like usual. If ever she needed a word from the Lord, it was now. Ignoring the tempting smell of coffee from downstairs, she curled up on the spacious window seat and opened the book in her lap.

Okay, Lord, you brought us this far. I was so sure I was doing the right thing last night when we ran. Now I'm having doubts. Should we have stayed and gone to the police? Would that have been better than running away? But David ran and I just felt sure that's what you were telling me to do when I read that scripture.

Peace rested gently on her shoulders as though God was saying, "You asked me what to do, I told you and you obeyed. Don't question yourself anymore."

Kristi smiled and continued her prayer. Thank you, Jesus. Thank you for our safe delivery. Now show us the next move that we need to make. Keep your protection around us. Go before us and keep the way safe. Thank you, Lord. Oh, and if you would stay behind us too in case those goons try to catch up with us, that would be great. If you would point them in another direction that would help too. Thank you for who you are. Thank you for loving us.

Kristi opened the Bible. Psalm 1. She cast her eyes heavenward. This is what you want me to read? She gave a small shrug and began with verse 1.

"Blessed is the man who walks not in the counsel of the ungodly, nor stands in the path of sinners, nor sits in the seat of the scornful; But his delight is in the law of the Lord, And in His law he meditates day and night. He shall be like a tree planted by the rivers of water, that brings forth its fruit in its season, Whose leaf also shall not wither; and whatever he does shall prosper."

Kristi frowned. What on earth does this have to do with anything, God? She kept reading praying for God to reveal what He wanted her to know.

Verse 4 said, "The ungodly are not so, but are like the chaff which the wind drives away. Therefore the ungodly shall not stand in the judgment, nor sinners in the congregation of the righteous. For the Lord knows the way of the righteous, But the way of the ungodly shall perish." So are you saying that we are walking the way you want? She smiled, Or rather, running the way you want? Which way, Lord? What now?

# # #

Curses rang in the deserted Walton home. It was 7:45 on Sunday morning. The man that David had dubbed "Moe" was furious. He and his partner had arrived last night around 11:30 to find the house empty. The family had run and "Moe" wanted to know who had tipped them off. Waiting around in the dark all night had not improved his disposition one bit.

Trashing the place had been the next item on his agenda if only to let off some steam. His partner had stopped him, so his frustration level was still running high. There wasn't even a dog to kick.

"Calm down, Mick, we'll catch them." This bored statement was from the other stooge, "Curly." David had probably dubbed him "Curly" because of the tight brown curls that clung to his head. A cigarette dangled between his fingers. Ashes floated carelessly on the royal blue carpet. No ashtrays in the house. Figured.

Mick sneered, "Oh really? What, you can read minds about where they're going now, Lyle?"

Lyle flicked more ashes then leaned his head against the back of the sofa. "Nope, can't read minds."

"So what now?"

"I can read a tracer, though."

This flat statement brought his partner up short. "Huh?"

An evil grin crossed Lyle's thin lips. "They're driving his car, aren't they? You know how they say money talks?" A ring of smoke made its way to the ceiling in a lazy motion. More ashes drifted down. He glanced at his watch. "Pretty soon, it'll be shouting. I'm just giving them time to get comfortable before we show up. In fact, I'd say they're probably pretty comfortable right about now."

A matching evil grin spread across the other man's face as he crossed his thick arms and leaned back against the doorjamb. "Yeah, comfortable. Then we shake them right out of comfort and into a coffin."

"According to the boss, that's the plan."

"What's the boss gonna get out of this anyway?"

"Beats me. I was just told to grab the kid whatever it took. Personally don't care why they want her, so long as I get my money."

"Yeah. And that suitcase full of fifty grand. Can't believe he took it and ran."

"That was stupid on our part. The only smart thing was putting that tracer in there. Shoulda known he wasn't gonna be bought off."

"Why not? All the others have. Haven't had no trouble outta them neither."

Lyle flicked another set of ashes to the carpet. "That's true. That's true. Well, they won't get far. We should have this all wrapped up by lunch time."

"Yeah, signed, sealed...and buried."

#

David felt itchy, like they needed to get on the road and get going. Only he didn't know where to go to. Kristi had read her bible and prayed for over an hour. Not wanting to intrude, David had stayed out of her way going by downstairs to see what there was to eat. He had slept through breakfast and was now starving. When Grace and his mother woke, they would be hungry too.

A quick trip to the kitchen found breakfast in the refrigerator as promised – ham biscuits and a gallon of milk. But best of all – the counter to his left held a whole pot of coffee. David inhaled the scent of the fresh brew and said a silent thanks to Mike.

He pulled out the plate of country ham biscuits and popped them in the microwave. While they were warming, he ignored the milk and poured himself a steaming cup of the hot brew.

Ahhhh…there's nothing like the first jolt of caffeine in the morning. David set the mug aside and examined the rest of the food. There were three boxes of cereal, fresh fruit, juice, bowls, spoons and napkins set out on the counter. Grace would love the Fruit Loops.

A newspaper sat nicely folded next to the microwave and David picked it up. They had made front page news. Great. His picture and Grace's beamed out at him. His blood began a slow boil. He recognized that picture as the one that sat on top of the TV in his den.

David squashed as much anger as possible and began to skim the article. It basically covered everything the newscaster had reported the night before. However, it did include interviews with other people who had been at the doctor's office. They all painted Grace as a healer.

The microwave beeped distracting him from the newspaper. His stomach growled, reminding him of his priorities. The biscuits were ready and David swallowed three of them practically whole. The rest he left out and headed back up the stairs to see who else was awake and hungry. He buried the newspaper in the bottom of the trash, hoping no one else would see it.

When he popped his head in the room Grace and his mother were sharing, he noticed the empty bed. The sound of running water told him where they were, so he crossed to the den to see if Kristi was interested in eating.

She was still sitting on the pulled out sofa bed, but her eyes were open and she greeted him warmly when he walked in. She said, "Good morning. Did you sleep okay?"

It was incredible how her smile seemed to make the whole room seem brighter. "Yes, thanks. Only that should be my question to you. You're the one that had the sofa bed."

Another bright smile. "I slept great."

An awkward silence ensued. David shuffled his feet and cleared his throat. "Um, I, uh, I guess I owe you an apology for last night. And a thank you too. You've risked a lot to help us and I was pretty much a grump - to put it nicely."

"Forget it."

David looked at her. Really looked at her. Red curls tumbled in waves around her heart shaped face. Devoid of make-up, sitting there in an old t-shirt and a pair of sweats, she looked about sixteen years old. He had to clear his throat again. "No. I don't think I can forget it. So, again, thank you. I'm grateful. But just one question."

A brief look of - something - flashed across her face, but before David could decipher the look, she was once again smiling at him. She simply said, "You're more than welcome. What's your question?"

"How did you know what was going down last night? How did you know to call and warn us? And how did you know my cell phone number?"

Kristi looked frozen for a moment, then gave a small laugh. "That's three questions. Which one do you want answered first?"

Was she stalling? David shrugged. "Whichever."

"To answer your first question, I have a friend who works for MiracleCorp. She overheard a conversation about you and your daughter, put two and two together and called me."

"But that doesn't explain how she knew that you knew us. From the doctor's office, I mean. It just doesn't fit."

David watched Kristi's shoulders lift in a slight shrug and her eyes slid to the bible she still held in her hands. "I don't know. Maybe she saw the news broadcast and put two and two together. I guess we can thank God for that one."

That explanation made sense – sort of. David decided to drop it for now; he would ask more later. She was hiding something, but he didn't feel like she was a threat to him or his family at this point. And besides, he was still hungry.

"So," he rubbed his hands together, "moving on. Would you like some breakfast?"

"Food! Yes, I'm starved. Lead on, oh grateful one."

"Funny."

"Yes, I can be sometimes."

"Do you think I'll ever get the last word?"

She laughed. "Not if I'm around."

"So, what were you reading this morning?" David changed the subject. He knew she had been having her quiet time. Guilt pierced him briefly. He hadn't had a quiet time since Lydia had died. When all of his praying and studying the bible and begging God to spare Lydia hadn't worked, David figured God just didn't have time to listen to one insignificant human being. So, he'd given up on God. If God didn't have time for him, David sure wasn't going to waste time trying to bend His almighty ear.

He glanced at Kristi who had a puzzled frown on her pretty face. She finally spoke thoughtfully. "It was kind of weird, actually. I usually pray before I read any passage of scripture asking God to teach me; to show me what he wants me to get out of the passage. I had never read this particular passage before so maybe that accounts for it, but this morning was kind of strange."

David was intrigued. "How so?"

"Well, the passage I read didn't seem to relate to anything except…" she paused, then sighed. "Well, why don't I just quote it for you? The first part of verse 1 said, Blessed is the man who walks not in the counsel of the ungodly, nor stands in the path of sinners, nor sits in the seat of the scornful."

At David's stunned look, she shrugged and said, "Photographic memory," as though it was no big deal. She went on. "That could mean…" Kristi stopped cold as though a thought had just come to her.

"What?"

She was thoughtful. "Um, never mind. Let me think on it some more and I'll get back to you on it."

David grasped her cold hand. "Hey, are you okay?"

"I'm not sure. Just feed me first, all right? And let me think."

David had no idea what was going on with her, but he decided to give her the space she requested.

And the food.

#

"Turn here." Mick watched the tracer light beam its steady signal. It hadn't moved since he'd turned it on early this morning and the two men were slowly closing in on the beacon.

"Now which way?" Lyle drove with careful precision. The needle on the speedometer never moved above the speed limit. No way was he getting stopped by some cop who hadn't met his quota for the month.

"Left, at the light. We're almost there."

"Are they still in the same place?" Lyle asked.

"Yup, they haven't budged. They must be pretty confident that they're safe, otherwise they'd be moving."

"I wonder where they spent the night. Everything's full around here. All I see are "No Vacancy" signs." Lyle's eyes moved constantly, never settling on any one place for long. He wasn't about to make a wrong turn and lose time. The boss was waiting.

Mick looked up from the tracking device. They were practically sitting on top of the little blinking dot. Now they just had to keep their eyes open and spot a Red Ford Explorer.

Lyle spotted a house. "Mick, what you think?" He pointed to the sign that read Mountain Home Bed and Breakfast.

"Gotta be it. Nothin' else around here except private homes. No hotels either."

"Do you see his car?" Lyle asked.

"No, just a couple of four doors - no SUVs. Pull around the back," Mick suggested. "There's probably extra parking back there and if he's got any brains at all, he's not gonna park right out front."

"Well, well. Would you look at that?" Lyle's evil grin made Mick shudder. Not much bothered Mick, but pure evil scared even him. Lyle spoke again. "I'm gonna pull back around to the front. Let's watch the place a bit and just kinda wait and see what's going on?"

"Why don't we just go on and in and grab 'em? They never lock these places up. We can catch them off guard."

Lyle swung a hand and landed a hard smack upside Mick's head. He growled, "Do you or do you not remember the orders?"

"Ow!" Mick rubbed the offended area and glared at his partner. "Yeah, I remember. No attention brought down on the foundation. I got it. I got it. Lay off the hittin', will ya?"

"Just trying to knock some sense in your thick head. You're such an idiot sometimes."

"And you're such a nice guy." Mick didn't bother to hide

his irritation or his sarcasm.

"Yeah, that's me, Mr. Nice Guy. There's all kinds of people in this place. We gotta play it cool, or they'll be calling in the cops." Lyle grunted as he shut off the engine.

"So why don't we just walk in the front door and ask for 'em?"

#

Kristi swallowed the last bite of ham biscuit and sat back with a sigh. David had gone back upstairs to check on his family while she finished eating...and thinking.

She had managed to squirm her way out of answering his questions for the most part, but most importantly, the question of how she knew his cell phone number. She had memorized the file she had been given by her boss when she was assigned to Grace.

But she wasn't about to tell David that. Yet.

Her quiet time was lingering in the recesses of her mind. She was still working over the verse in her mind, but she thought she knew what the Lord was trying to tell her.

The counsel of the ungodly certainly could refer to her bosses. The path of sinners could be another reference to said employers and - if she was honest - herself. Basically everything in the verses said she was not to return to her job. She definitely did not want to be on the same path as people who would kill.

The decision to quit was pretty much a no-brainer after seeing what the company she had been so loyal and faithful to had been capable of doing. She just hated that she'd been a part of it for this long. Why had she not seen it before? Had she been so focused on trying to get close to her sister and brother-in-law that she had been blind to the company's evil?

"Hi there." Kristi jumped, her thoughts scattered. It was Mike. She said, "Oh, hello there. You startled me."

"Sorry about that. I just came down to check that you guys found everything okay." His words were clipped; not rude, just northern. Kristi smiled at her stereotyping.

"Yes, thank you so much. We slept great and breakfast was delicious."

Mike beamed down at her. "Good, good. So how long you think you'll need the rooms?"

Kristi frowned. She really hadn't thought that far ahead. Running into the night and trying to stay two steps ahead of killers had one living for the moment, not thinking too far into the future.

"I'm not really sure."

"Is...everything all right with you guys?"

Kristi's startled gaze met his. It was sympathetic, concerned. "Um, yes. We're...fine."

"Well, you seem like nice people. If you need any help just let me know." He turned to go.

"Wait." When Mike turned back to her, she licked her lips, then decided to chance it. "We haven't done anything illegal - or wrong. But for reasons better left unsaid, some people are trying to track us down. The little girl especially. If someone should come looking for us - some official looking men flashing important badges and sporting dark sunglasses - could you stall them as long as possible without getting yourself in trouble?"

Mike's eyes flared with surprise at the unusual request and Kristi wondered for a moment if she had spoken erroneously, but then he simply narrowed his eyes and answered, "Sure, I can do that."

She breathed easier. "Thanks."

Reaching into the back pocket of the thick designer sweatpants, she pulled out her credit card. An uneasy feeling flitted through her at the idea of using it, but they had to pay the man and it might be that they hadn't figured out she was with David and Grace. So maybe they wouldn't be

tracking her credit card use. Yet. They'd figure it out soon
enough though. "Just put last night on it. Are the rooms still
available tonight should we need them?"

"Yep. You just take your time and let me know."

"Great. Thanks so much."

Mike swiped the card and handed it back to her. "No
problem. We enjoy having nice guests like yourself. I'm
heading back over to the house. My little girl had a bad case
of chicken pox, at least we thought she did."

"What do you mean?" Kristi held her breath fearing she
already knew the answer.

"Funny thing was, by the time I got back to the house
last night and checked on her, she was fine."

"Fine?" she squeaked.

"Yup. Fine. You wouldn't know anything about that
would you?"

Kristi gulped. "Ah, yeah. Yes, I would. Wow."

"Yeah, I saw the news this morning - and the paper. I figured you might know what was going on."

Kristi decided to just lay it on the line. "They think
Grace can heal. They want her for testing. David turned
them down. They were going to kill him and grab Grace.
That's why we're running. You won't turn us in will you?"

"After what that sweet little girl did for my baby? No
way."

Kristi huffed a sigh of relief. "Oh thank you."

Mike waved as he backed out of the door. "Like I said,
you let me know if you need anything else."

Kristi thanked him one more time, took a last swig of
orange juice, grabbed two more biscuits to eat, and headed
back upstairs to figure out what the plan was.

"Hi Ms. Henderson." Kristi turned at the voice coming
from the little girl standing in the doorway of the bedroom.
Her heart immediately melted to see that sweet, innocent
smile. But she couldn't help blinking at the blue eyes. My

goodness, thought Kristi, they are something else - entrancing. She smiled at Grace. "Hello, sweet pea. Did you sleep well?" Blond curls bounced an affirmative answer. "And are you hungry?" Another affirmative blond bounce. Kristi held out her hand. "Come on, then, let's get you a biscuit from downstairs then. Where's your daddy?"

"The shower."

Kristi didn't hear the water running, so he must have just finished. She walked over to speak through the door. "David, I'm going to take Grace downstairs to get her something to eat, okay?"

His head popped around the door. He eyed her or a moment, then said, "Sure, thanks."

"I'm coming too." Nancy walked out of the den. As the trio began their descent, Kristi heard the front door open.

She paused on the step; senses on high alert. Why she was instantly alarmed, she wasn't sure, but she couldn't figure out who would be coming in at this time on a Sunday morning.

Telling herself she was being paranoid, she nevertheless, cautiously peeked around the edge of the wall where she could see the front door, but whoever had just walked in couldn't see her.

What she saw made her slap a hand over her mouth to cover the gasp. She recognized the men now standing in the doorway having seen them in the halls at work.

How had they found them?

Chapter 6

"How can I help you folks?" Mike stepped in around the two "men in black." As he did, his eyes met Kristi's for a brief moment. She hadn't realized she had come down the steps as far as she had and immediately pulled back. One of the men spoke up.

"We're looking for a man on the run with his mother and little girl." Kristi heard papers rustling. "Have you seen them?" He must have pulled a photograph out of an envelope. Kristi frowned and tried to think over her pounding heart.

"What have they done?" She heard Mike answer the question with one of his own.

"The dad's name is David Walton, the little girl is Grace. He's stolen $50,000 from us and we want it back."

A different voice that must have belonged to the partner piped in. "Their car is parked outside. They must be around here somewhere. Is it all right if we have a look around?"

"Well, sure, I guess. You guys might want to check the dining room first. We just finished up breakfast."

Kristi just about jumped out of her skin when she felt the hand on her arm. She looked up to see David's white, pinched face staring into hers. He placed a finger against his lips and motioned for her to follow him. Kristi looked around to see Grace and Nancy were already gone. She hadn't heard them leave.

With a silent nod, Kristi followed David back into the den area and over to the window. A fire escape. Kristi shoved the two biscuits into her purse; she'd clean out the crumbs later. Grace would still be hungry and she had no idea when they would be able to stop for something to eat.

David leaned over to whisper in her ear. "Mom and Grace are in your car along with the bags. Here's your purse." Kristi swung the bag over her shoulder. David continued whispering, "Just drive them somewhere safe. I don't know what I was thinking. I should have done this last night. I'm going to take mine to a storage area, so I'll call you when I dump it and you can come pick me up. Right now they don't realize you're with us, so they're not looking for your car."

"Okay."

She had started out the window when he stopped her. The intensity of his gaze stole her breath. "My child is my life," he said. "I'm trusting you with my life."

Kristi swallowed hard. How was she going to tell this man that she was the one who had helped put his life in danger? She'd have to worry about that later. She looked him straight in the eye. "You can trust me. I promise."

He hesitated one short moment before leaning over to place a soft kiss on her forehead. "Thank you."

Kristi couldn't have moved if she wanted to. His totally innocent kiss had sent her heart into overdrive. But then he gave her a gentle shove and she was on the first step. David was right behind her.

She got her equilibrium back and clambered down the fire escape going as quickly and quietly as possible, her purse banging against her back. At the bottom, she hung for a brief moment then dropped lightly to the ground. She heard and felt the gravel crunch under her feet.

Thank goodness they had parked their cars around the

back. David gave her hand a brief squeeze before heading to his Explorer.

"Wait!" David and Kristi turned as one toward his mother. She was hurrying toward the Explorer. Her hand held out, she demanded, "Give me the keys. I've been doing a lot of thinking and praying. I'm going to visit Helena in Italy."

Kristi watched David balk at the proclamation. "No way, Mom."

His mother's blue eyes - so much like David's - flashed. "We don't have a lot of time to stand around debating. I'm going. Now give me the keys. I'll find a way to get in touch with you."

"Mom?" Indecision was written all over his handsome face.

Nancy Walton snatched the keys from her son's hand. Opening the door, she pulled out the briefcase that held the money and shoved it into her son's hands. "I'll be in touch. Take care." She blinked back the tears. "You take care of my grandbaby - and yourself. If you get yourself killed, I don't know what I'll do."

David reached out to grab her in a quick bear hug. "We'll be all right. It's you I'm worried about. Please be careful."

Nancy returned the hug, then pushed him away. "They'll be out here any minute. Now scram."

Then she was in the car and pulling out of the driveway.

"Hey! There they go!" A man shouted from the window on the second floor.

David and Kristi exchanged a frightened look and climbed quickly into Kristi's waiting Suburban. She gunned the engine and turned onto the side street that led to the highway. "Are they following us?" Kristi threw the question at David

"No, they're following Mom." Fear lanced through

every word.

"Daddy?"

Kristi looked in the rear view mirror at the sound of the small voice. Grace was looking pretty wide-eyed – and scared. David answered his daughter. "Yes, sweetie?"

"Where's my Granma going? Is she coming back?" The lower lip trembled. Poor baby.

Kristi saw David briefly shut his eyes before he hastened to reassure the little girl. "Of course she is. She's got to put the Explorer somewhere because we don't need two cars. Then she's going to visit Auntie Helena in Italy for a little while. But she'll be back. Okay?"

Relief flashed. If her daddy said it, it would happen. "Okay."

Kristi was reminded in those few moments of unabashed vulnerability that in spite of her incredible gift and eyes that made her seems years older, she was still just a six-year-old little girl who needed the security of the two constants in her life - her daddy and her grandmother.

Kristi looked in her rear view mirror. They weren't being followed - yet. It was just a matter of time before they figured out Kristi was involved in helping the Walton's escape - especially when she didn't show up for work tomorrow morning. She heaved a sigh. Well, Monday had never been her favorite day anyway. Quitting her job on a Sunday afternoon just meant one less Monday she had to work.

At least that was one way of looking at it.

She turned to David and said, "We've got to come up with something that will get these goons off out tails and out of our lives - permanently."

"No kidding. Think. What do these people do for a living?"

Kristi scoffed and said, "Apparently anything that will get them what they want - including sending hired guns to kill when they don't get their way."

"Exactly. And do you think that we're the first ones to cross them?"

Kristi wasn't slow; his thinking was coming in loud and clear. "No," she drew the word out, "most likely not."

"So, if we could somehow get together with someone who lived to tell about crossing MiracleCorp, we could possibly get some kind of material together that would expose the whole crooked corporation - and once exposed, they would have no reason to come after Grace."

"True. But how do we go about finding out that information?" Kristi was getting into his plan. The same plan was forming in her mind now. "Wait a minute! I bet Tess could help us out."

"Tess? Who's that?"

"My best friend and co-worker. She's the one who called me and told me that I needed to warn you about what those goons were up to. She's our inside information source."

"Co-worker?"

Kristi froze as she realized what she let slip. She heaved a sigh. She was left with no choice but to tell him the truth – or at least part of it. "I...used to work at MiracleCorp."

"Come again?"

Kristi ran a hand through her curls and made a one-handed turn onto a small back road that led to the highway. How much did she reveal? She couldn't lose his trust now. He needed her more than he knew and if she told him everything, he'd dump her on the side of the road - and she really wouldn't blame him. "I used to work there. I was recruited while still in my residency at Greensburg Regional. It sounded like a great job. I really thought I was helping people."

"You work for the people that are trying to kill us?" David's voice was low; anger was woven through his words like a steel thread.

"Worked, David. As in past tense." Kristi didn't tell

him that her official last day had been this past Friday. Two days ago.

"So, that's how your connection - Tess, I believe you called her - knew to call you. Your co-worker. Your inside track." Kristi heard the rage building and fought to think of a way to derail it.

"David, if I wanted you dead, you'd be dead. Instead, I'm risking my life for you. What more do I have to do to prove that I only want to see you and Grace safe?"

Her quiet question apparently threw him into confusion because he said no more; just closed his eyes and leaned his head back against the headrest.

"Tell me about MiracleCorp." His question came out of left field and for a moment Kristi wondered if she had imagined it. He spoke into her thoughts, "Well?"

She hadn't imagined it. "What do you want to know?"

"I'm not sure...just start talking about it and I'll ask you a question if I need clarification on anything."

Kristi took a deep breath and blew it out slowly. "Okay...history...MiracleCorp was founded in 1989 by Dr. James M. Sinclair. Its primary philosophy is to provide "miracles" for those less fortunate – the poor, the uninsured, the homeless, those who have a need and can't afford it."

"Isn't that what Medicaid is for?"

"Yes, of course, but this went beyond that. For example- a poor young child from a single parent household is diagnosed with a terminal illness – and no insurance. Dr. Sinclair is informed of this – through whatever means - and arranges for this child to be brought to MiracleCorp Hospital. There, the patient receives the best medical care from the best doctors recruited from all over the world. Not only that, but he and his mother are given the means to go on the vacation of their dreams. All expenses paid to Disney World or some such wonderful trip."

"Hence the name MiracleCorp."

"Yes, to a point."

"Sounds like the Make a Wish foundation."

"That's basically what it is, only we provide the medical care to go along with it."

"So, what is Dr. Sinclair getting out of all of this? And how did we end up with those goons on our tail?"

Kristi sighed. She knew why the goons were on their tail, but didn't really know why Dr. Sinclair wanted Grace so badly. Was there a particular reason he wanted her within his grasp so quickly?

She answered the first of David's questions, ignoring the last. "I really wish I knew. As far as I knew when I joined MiracleCorp, I was just helping dying families live 'normally' for one last time. I was part of the team at the hospital that took care of the patients. After a while, I moved to the lab. I needed a change from the constant sorrow – and inevitable death that followed."

"So where is all this coming from? What's the connection to Grace and me? Why do they want her for testing? What does her gift have to do with them?" His anger had been diffused for the moment. Confusion reigned in its place.

Kristi hedged. "Now that's the million dollar question, isn't it?"

David patted his briefcase and murmured, "Actually, it's the $50,000 question."

# # #

"They turned there, you idiot! Turn around before you lose them." Lyle reached over from the passenger seat and punched Mick in the arm. The car swerved into a U-turn then made a quick left.

The red Explorer was a few yards ahead, but still in sight.

"You think they're all in there? All I see is one head."

"He's probably got 'em ducked down in case we start shooting."

"Yeah." Left hand on the wheel, Mick reached over with his right and pulled the gun from its hiding place in the glove compartment. "Guess he ain't so dumb after all."

Lyle swore. "Well you are if you think you can start shooting and not kill the kid. No way can we let anything happen to her. Put that thing away. Remember, boss said low profile. No shooting in the daytime."

"I'm almost up to the car. You want me to run it off the road?"

"Yeah, give it a good bump."

Mick pushed the gas pedal and roared up behind the Walton vehicle. He slammed into the back of it, spinning the steering wheel to maneuver around the Explorer. Whoever was driving was either a good driver or extremely lucky. The car only swerved left, then back into the lane. It picked up speed, obviously trying to outrun them, so Mick decided to get up beside it this time and run it completely off the road.

There was only one problem when he came up beside it. "Hey, Lyle, it's the old woman driving!"

"What?" Lyle banged his hand on the dash and cursed. "Get up there again and let me have a look." Sure enough, the old lady's frightened eyes peered into his. The rest of the car looked empty. Lyle swore again, then ordered, "Run it off the road. We'll grab her and she can tell us where they are."

Lyle's statement made Mick pause for a brief moment before he lifted a shoulder in a shrug. "She'll probably have a heart attack, but all right, whatever you..."

The noise cut off the rest of his sentence. It sounded like a freight train. Were there tracks around here? Mick slammed on the brakes and skidded to a halt. He watched the Explorer swerve, rock, then gain control as it sped down the highway.

"Get out of here!" The fear in the scream shook Mick out of his current befuddlement over where the noise was coming from. When he looked in the rearview mirror, horrified understanding of his partner's fear thumped through him.

A gray cloud was rapidly moving towards them. Swirling, twirling, and destroying everything in its path, the thunderous mass moved steadily closer. Along with the deafening roar, debris and dirt were flying - and the sedan and its occupants were right in the path of the oncoming, spinning funnel.

"Get us out of here, man. Find a ditch or a bridge or something, but get us out of here! We'll never survive a hit."

Mick didn't have to be told twice. Not bothering to glance back, he floored the pedal and the car shot forward. Wind bounced the car, giving to meaning to the phrase, "rock and roll."

Mick was able to keep ahead of it, but barely. The speedometer read ninety miles per hour, then a hundred. No longer the ones in pursuit, they raced for their lives. The turnoff for the Interstate was just ahead – along with an overpass. It was their only hope.

The funnel was relentless in its chase, a merciless predator stalking its prey.

Mick dared a glance in the mirror and gasped. It was right on them!

"Come on, come on! Faster! Faster!"

He could barely hear his partner's scream over the roar. "I've got it to the floor!" he yelled back.

And he did, but it didn't matter.

The funnel of wind won the race.

# # #

Kristi turned into the hotel parking lot and threw the car into park. Two hours later, in Knoxville, Tennessee, it was time to hole up for a while and figure out how they were going to get out of this mess.

Grace was asleep and David looked to be in deep thought. She hadn't yet told him about Grace healing the little girl, Sylvia. She'd save that one for when he wasn't' so tired and could possibly handle it.

"David, is this okay?"

David blinked twice, then his gaze focused on their surroundings. "Sure. Why not? I'll go check us in. Will you wait with Grace?" He opened the door.

"Of course. Uh...David?" Kristi stopped him.

"Yeah?" He leaned down to look back in the car.

"What are you going to pay with? I really don't think we should use the cash. It's probably marked. They'll ask for a credit card." She hated to bring it up, but it was a real concern. David's tired expression sat heavy on her heart. If only she..., but now was not the time for recriminations.

"Here," she dug the card out of the storage compartment between the two front seats, "use this one."

"But...," he started to protest.

"It's in my name. Hopefully, they won't connect us if they start asking questions around here."

"Are you sure?"

She smiled at him. When his eyes weren't shooting sparks at her, they made the butterflies in her stomach swoop and soar. "I'm sure."

"Thanks. I'll pay you back as soon as we get this mess cleaned up." David's tone warned her not to argue.

"No problem." Agreeing was easier for the moment. Right now it didn't matter. If they ended up dead, it was a moot point anyway.

After his broad back disappeared into the hotel lobby, Kristi looked around to see Grace still sleeping soundly. She reached over to flip on the radio, turning the volume low in order not to wake the little girl.

"...an unexplained tornado that basically came from out of nowhere and disappeared just as fast. There were two casualties. The car these two individuals were riding in was right in the path of the tornado. Their names have just been released. Lyle Gentry and Mick Richards. The two men were employed with MiracleCorp. As you well know, this is a company that was founded and now managed by CEO, James Mark Sinclair. Dr. Sinclair will express his sympathy to the families of these gentlemen in a press conference in approximately thirty minutes."

Kristi broke out in a cold sweat. Her bible reading from this morning came to mind with clarity. The ungodly are not so, but are like the chaff which the wind drives away. Lord? Did you do that? Drive them away with the wind? Wow, oh, wow, God, please don't let James have anything to do with all this – or Pamela....

"Where's my daddy?" The sleepy voice grabbed Kristi's attention from her prayer.

"Hey, sleepyhead." She turned to gaze into the back seat and couldn't help smiling at the little girl. "He's gone to get us a room."

"Oh." Grace looked out the window, then back at Kristi. "Why were those men chasing us?"

Kristi bit her lip. How did she answer that one? "Well," she drew the word out slowly as she thought, "they want something that we don't want them to have."

Blue eyes peered into Kristi's. The little girl studied her for a moment before sadness crept across her face. "They want me don't they?"

The wisdom behind the question stunned Kristi speechless. She felt her mouth moving, but couldn't seem to get words past her lips. Finally, she just shut them.

Grace looked down at her hands. "It's because people get well when I pray for them, isn't it?"

God, help! What do I tell her?

Fortunately David chose that time to show up and Kristi breathed a sigh of relief when he said, "Okay, I got us a couple of rooms. There's an adjoining door."

"Great." Kristi winced at her overly bright response. David raised an eyebrow. Kristi just ignored him. She'd tell him about the conversation with Grace later. Fortunately the little girl was distracted. "Hey Daddy, do they have an indoor pool? Can we go swimming?"

"We'll see, honey." Typical parental response to avoid saying no. Kristi smiled at the small moment of normalcy.

Quickly, they gathered their things and headed for the rooms. Once they were settled, hopefully, they'd be able to figure out the next move in this complicated game of chess. And hopefully that move wouldn't land them in checkmate.

# # #

The glass shattered against the wall. Liquid ran down the paneling to puddle on the floor. James grabbed his throbbing head and groaned as he pictured the look on his wife's face when he told her he had failed – again. Why was it so hard to catch three people? If he didn't know better, he'd swear God was sitting up there laughing at his futile attempts to save his son.

James lifted a clenched fist and shook it at the ceiling. "This is all your fault! You could do something. You owe me! I've dedicated my life to working for you and this is the thanks I get? Well, I don't appreciate it and I don't appreciate you. Go find some other stooge to play games with; just leave me alone!" The last word was wrung out on another groan.

Anger was like bitter medicine on his tongue. But instead of healing, it poisoned him with a slow burn. He no longer wanted to go home to see his family. Helplessness plagued him night and day. Pamela no longer pleaded with him to do something. Seth no longer looked at him with hope in his eyes.

Instead, they just looked whipped. No hope, no energy, no…nothing. And now, his only chance was lost. Seth's only chance gone.

A little girl with healing powers.

Before Seth's illness, James would have scoffed at the thought of believing such a person could exist. Now he wavered between railing at the Almighty in anger at the injustice of it all and praying that he would find the little girl in time. Never had he felt such a loss of control – not just over his life and his family, but over his emotions.

James prided himself on his self-control. Now that pride cowered, whimpering in the corner. When the phone rang, he just stared at it, blinking slowly. He had no desire to end his tantrum just yet, but the thought that it might be Geoff saying that he'd found the girl had him unable to resist reaching over to grab the handset. He took a deep breath before he answered, "Sinclair here."

"Hi James." It was Geoff. "As you know, Lyle and Mick were killed in that freaky tornado accident, but I've got two more guys tracking them down. We should have her in less than twenty-four hours. Tell Seth to keep hanging on."

"I will. And Geoff?"

"Yeah?"

"I really hope she's not another…dud, for want of a better word. Make sure your sources are accurate on this one okay?"

"What's that supposed to mean, James?"

James sighed loudly into the phone. He really didn't know either. "Nothing, Geoff. Nothing. Just get her and her family here safe, okay? No tests, no playing around. Bring her straight to me and straight to Seth."

"But James…," Geoff started to protest.

James interrupted, "I'm serious about this. Bring her

straight here. Seth doesn't have time to wait around while you waste time in your precious lab. And plus, I want her alive. I don't know what happened to the other people you found, but somehow they managed to disappear before stepping foot in this house. That's not going to happen again, understood?"

Geoff didn't speak at first. When he did, James could tell it was with an effort that he wasn't shouting. "Understood." Geoff disconnected them before James could say another word. James clicked the cordless off, then set it on the base. Geoff would be all right, he assured himself. And even if he wasn't all right, frankly, he didn't have time to worry about it. Geoff's days, possibly hours weren't numbered. He could worry about his brother later. Right now, finding Grace to heal his son consumed James' every thought; defined his purpose for existing. Seth topped the priority list; and at this moment, Geoff didn't even rank in the top ten.

Geoff clutched the receiver and forced himself to place it calmly back on the base. Heaving it to smash against the wall was the more appealing option, but then he'd have to pick up the pieces - and he was doing enough of that already.

Seth. Grace. James didn't know what he was asking. Finding this child seemed to be an impossible act. It was like she had something watching over her, guarding her, keeping his men from getting close to her.

Did she? Geoff didn't get into the spiritual stuff much, but this was getting ridiculous. Never had he had this much trouble locating one person. And now he had caught James reading his Bible more than once lately. James also liked to try out his new knowledge on Geoff and often asked Geoff questions to which he had no answers.

And Seth. Every time Geoff walked in to that bedroom

and saw the shrunken, deformed body, he wanted to vomit. He remembered when a young, healthy Seth used to run into his arms.

"Unca Geoff, Unca Geoff!" Seth plowed into Geoff's legs and Geoff reached down to swing him high. Little boy squeals and delighted laughter squeezed his heart, but not with the joy one would expect him to feel, but with sorrow, anger and bitterness. He hugged Seth and put him down to run on his way, but the anger lingered, swirling in his mind and his heart. So that Geoff could only think one thought.

"He should have been mine." Geoff's own voice jerked him out of his thoughts and back to his mission.

Find Grace.

He reached for the phone with one hand dialed with the other. When the cool voice answered, Geoff didn't bother with pleasantries. "You find out where they are yet?" he barked into the phone, impatient with the unknown. Helplessness was not a feeling that he was used to. He was used to feeling powerful and in control. Now he had to rely on others to carry out his orders. He didn't like the feeling.

The voice answered, "No sir, not yet, but we're working on it. We'll let you know as soon as we find out anything."

"See that you do. And see that you don't fail again." He hung up the phone and stared at the photograph on his desk. Seth, Pamela and James. One big happy family. Oh, yeah, he'd find Grace. He had to find her. Soon.

#

David threw the pen down and rubbed his eyes. "You got anything for a headache? Whatever air freshener stuff they spray in these places is a migraine waiting to happen."

Kristi, perched on the edge of the bed, looked up from her laptop. "Yes, I think there's something in my overnight bag next door. I'll get it for you."

"Thanks. I'm getting a monster of one." David rubbed the back of his neck. No doubt about it. The stress was getting to him.

David watched Kristi cross the room to the connecting door and disappear. He shut his eyes and didn't open them until she returned. He didn't hear her, but the scent of strawberries told him she was back.

"Here." Her voice was soft; the sympathy oozing from the one word did wonders for his disposition.

Gratefully, he took at the two little white pills from Kristi's outstretched palm. She held a cup of water in her other hand. And she smelled like strawberries again. David inhaled deeply and the pain in his head eased somewhat. He took the cup, tossed the pills back and took a gulp of the water. Hopefully the medicine would get rid of the rest of the ache.

When she sat down in the chair beside him, the small round table in the corner of the room seemed to become even smaller. Her proximity drowned out the movie playing in the background. Grace was engrossed in the antics of Bob and Larry, her favorite Veggie Tales characters.

"It's amazing to me that people can get rich off of a talking tomato and cucumber," Kristi murmured with amusement.

David gave an answering chuckle. "Yeah, thank God for good videos."

Thank God for good videos. Thank God he had thought to throw a couple in her suitcase. Thank God for well-equipped hotel rooms and VCR's. David realized that he was thanking God an awful lot.

God is always here, David. You've just got to reach out to take His hand. Lydia's voice rang with clarity in his tired mind. The memory of his wife shot a pang through his heart. It startled him, but only because the pang wasn't as sharp as it had been just a few days before.

The thought made him look at the beautiful woman sitting beside him. Did he need to thank God for her too? Anger stirred within and he felt guilty. How could he be thanking God for anything? Wasn't it His fault that his daughter no longer has a woman to call 'mommy'? Wasn't it His fault that his child's life was in danger and they were on the run? After all, hadn't He given her this…gift? Curse?

"Okay. I think I know how to work this."

"Huh?" Her voice brought him to the task before them. "Work what?"

"We've got to find the other people that have been contacted by MiracleCorp because they thought that these people had some kind of special powers or something. We've agreed that Grace can't be the only one; there's got to be others." She rubbed her forehead, then brushed a few stray hairs away from her eyes. David was shocked to realize he wanted the right to do that for her.

Focus, man. He cleared his throat. "Okay. How are we going to even start getting that kind of information?"

"Tess."

"Your friend?"

"Yeah." The word was drawn out on a sigh.

"What's wrong?"

"Nothing really. I was thinking that if anyone could find the stuff we needed it would be her. She's worked there a lot longer than I have and she has a higher level security clearance. I just don't want to do anything that's going to cause her any trouble."

"Security clearance? What does a place like MiracleCorp need with security clearance?"

Kristi's forehead crinkled again. "I don't really know. I guess with all the testing and stuff that goes on there – especially in the lab - maybe there are competitors who would want to steal information from them." Her delicate shoulders lifted in a half-shrug. "I've never really thought about it."

"Why don't you call Tess and see if she's willing to help us. Once we learn that, then we'll know how to move forward."

"What time is it?"

David glanced at his watch. "Two thirty."

"Today's Sunday. She'll be at her parent's house with her new boyfriend. They'll have just finished lunch and if there's a football game on, they'll be watching it." A soft smile crossed her lips as she thought about her friends. David envied her closeness. Since Lydia's death two years ago, he'd lost contact with most of their friends.

Oh, be honest with yourself, he chided silently, you've deliberately shut everyone out of your life. It had just seemed easier to make it through each day without seeing people that reminded him of life with Lydia. Grace was reminder enough. Would anyone even miss him?

Being a self-employed carpenter had its advantages, but it didn't make for much socialization. No, no one would miss him until a customer called to check on a late order and no one returned the call. It could be days, even weeks before someone figured out something was wrong. Unless, of course, someone figured it out from that newscast last night – which was highly likely. And since he and his mother homeschooled Grace, no one would really miss her any time soon either. Certainly not the church they'd stopped attending two years ago.

"David," Kristi's soft voice broke into his thoughts.

He looked up at her. "Yeah?"

"Before I call Tess, I...need to tell you something, but I'm not sure exactly how to tell you." She stumbled around the words.

"What do you mean?" David was curious, but not sure he liked the troubled look on her face. "What's it about?"

"About Grace...and Sylvia, that little girl of the Innkeeper's."

David felt foreboding descend upon him. "I probably don't want to hear this, do I?"

Kristi blew out a sigh, then dropped the bomb on him. "Grace overheard him say that his little girl was sick and offered to pray for her. She did and she healed that little girl of the chicken pox."

David drew a hand through is already rumpled hair. "No, she didn't. She couldn't have."

Kristi walked over to him and placed a hand on his shoulder. "Yes, she did. I talked with Mike this morning. He knew who Grace was when he came over. He confronted me with it and I didn't lie. I told him why we were on the run. He said he wouldn't turn us in."

"Yeah, he seems like a good man. So she healed his daughter. How did that work, Kristi? She wasn't in the same room...or even the same house with the child."

Kristi walked over to peek around the heavy curtains into the empty street beyond. Now if it would only stay that way. She turned to answer David and said, "I don't know, David. I've been thinking about it. I can't even to begin to try to fathom how God works. I just know He does work. There's a story in the book of Luke. I think it's chapter seven."

"What's it about?" David couldn't seem to help himself. Every time he talked to Kristi, it seemed he learned something new about the God he was coming back to.

"It's about a man - a centurion in the Roman army. It's weird this story is so fresh in my mind. I read it just a few days ago." She closed her eyes to bring up the words she had recently studied. "The man sent Jewish elders to Jesus to ask him to come and heal the servant."

"Why did he send elders? Why not go himself?"

"Well, you know the hatred that existed between the Romans and the Jews. The man himself obviously knew that the Jews possessed God's message for mankind. It says that he had a love for the nation and that he built the synagogue. So, it was natural that he would turn to Jesus in his time of need. He was also smart enough to know that he didn't want to disrupt a Jewish gathering."

"Okay, so what's any of this got to do with what happened with Grace?"

"Shush, I'm getting to that part."

David shushed and decided he could listen to her smooth voice all night - even if she was talking about God.

Kristi went on. "If you think about it, as the leader who delegates responsibility, the Roman soldier realized that he didn't need to be present for his orders to be carried out, he just told his men what to do and they did it - in the same way that Jesus didn't need to be present to heal his servant. And Jesus was amazed at this man's faith. In fact I think the verse says, 'When Jesus heard this, He was amazed at him, and turning to the crowd following him, he said, 'I will tell you, I have not found such great faith even in Israel.'"

Kristi paused to look at David. He indicated that she had his full attention and he wanted her to continue, so she went on. "I mean, this was absolutely amazing to Jesus that this man who was hated by the Jews could have displayed such faith. Jesus then told the crowd that many religious Jews would not enter the kingdom of heaven because of their lack of faith. They were religious, true, but they put so much store by their religious practices that they didn't have room for Christ and his new message. A message that basically says, don't limit God. And when we have a lack of faith, we limit God's ability to work through us."

"Wow." David could only stare at this amazing woman who knew so much and wasn't afraid to share it.

"Yeah, and apparently your daughter has the faith of a Roman Centurion."

"Or the Centurion had the faith of a child."

The profound statement left Kristi without words.

David closed his eyes, only to open them to stare at his precious child and say, "I want to believe, Kristi, I want that kind of faith, but I...I don't think I could stand it if something happened to Grace. I just don't know what to think about this healing gift. It's driving me absolutely nuts!" Emotion clogged his throat; his nose stung.

"I know, David. It's easy for me to sit here and spout about faith to you when I struggle with it in certain areas of my life too."

"What's wrong, Daddy?"

David looked over his shoulder to see Grace's attention had shifted from Larry and Bob to Kristi and him. He held out an arm and Grace slid next to his side and allowed David to squeeze her. "Nothing sweetheart. Just trying to figure out what to do next." David paused, then said, "You prayed for that little girl with the chicken pox, didn't you?"

Grace looked at the floor, but nodded. She whispered, "I'm sorry, Daddy."

David wanted to weep. His baby was apologizing for something that was not her fault - but felt like she had to offer an apology anyway. David pulled her even closer and dropped a kiss on her freshly washed curls. "It's okay, honey. You didn't do anything wrong." He paused, then, "You know she got all better, don't you?"

Grace lifted her head and offered him a small grin. "Yes, I know. God did it. He likes it when people ask for His help."

"Yes He does, doesn't He?" David gave her another squeeze and a pat on the back. He wished he felt like he could ask for God's help in this situation he now found himself. "Go back to the TV and don't worry, we'll figure something out." David blew out a sigh and looked up when he felt a hand on his shoulder.

Kristi said, "Let's take one step at a time. Let's call Tess."

"Do you think she'll help us?"

Kristi shrugged and reached for the phone. "Only one way to find out."

Chapter 7

"**D**id you find it, yet?" The tall black clad figure drummed impatient fingers on the roof of the demolished car. The sedan had been towed to the junkyard and was finally cleared for the owner to claim any items left behind.

The two men were only interested in one thing.

"Yep." His partner grunted as he backed out of what used to be the front seat. The blood on the shattered windshield didn't seem to faze him in the least. "Looks like it might have survived the tornado – or whatever kind of wind that was. Weirdest thing I ever heard of."

"Yeah, whatever. Give it here." Without waiting for the other man to hand it over, he simply reached out and took it. However, when he tried to pop the lid, it wouldn't budge. He spit out a flaming curse. "It's jammed. Here," he shoved it back at his partner, "take it and let's go. We'll figure out how to get it open later."

"Wait. Hold on. Yep. Got it." Triumph oozed from the shorter of the two men. The box opened and after he flipped a small switch it began to emit small blipping sounds. "Ah, music to my ears. It still works."

"Which way?"

"West."

"What were these idiots doing going south?" The disgust

in his voice made no secret about how he felt about the two men who had lost their lives in the tornado.

"Who knows? Looks to me like they didn't even have it on."

"Whatever." He had lost interest in the conversation. "Let's go west."

The two men climbed into a sedan that used to be identical to the one that now resembled a crushed soda can.

"How far away are they, Guthrie?" The taller man adjusted the seat to fit his long legs.

"Looks to be about three hours give or take a few minutes."

"Three hours. That'll put us in about Knoxville, Tennessee, won't it?"

"Yep." Guthrie adjusted a knob on the device.

"Three hours. In three hours - plus the time it takes to track them down - we can call our boss and tell him he's got a miracle on the way to see him. Let's get the job done."

"You want me to go ahead and give him a call and let him know what's going on?"

"Yeah, sure, let's do that."

Guthrie pulled out the cell phone and punched in a number. After the second ring, a gruff voice barked a greeting. Guthrie responded, "We've got a lead on the people you're looking for. We should have your miracle in sight within three hours or so. However, we'll probably wait until morning to make the grab. What do you want us to with her when we get her? Right. What about the dad and the old lady? You got it." He snapped the phone shut and turned to the driver. "He said to hold onto her. He wants to take care of the girl himself. He did say not to hurt the others if at all possible."

"Whatever the boss wants." He wheeled the sedan west; a hunter stalking its prey.

"Yep, whatever James Sinclair wants, James Sinclair gets."

#

"Hi Tess. How's the game going? Your team winning?"

"Kristi!" The exclamation was filled with relief. "Where are you? Are you okay? What about the Waltons? Are they okay?"

Despite the situation, Kristi almost laughed. Tess never did stop to get an answer before rushing into another question. The fact that she was a marvelous doctor was a miracle in itself. The doctor in Tess knew how to sit back, listen and observe. When the lab coat came off, it was like she became another person – or her true personality was able to emerge.

"We're fine – for now," Kristi soothed, "but if you hadn't given us that warning, I shudder to think what would have happened to David and Grace."

"Things are going to be crazy around work. I'm going to have to see if I can fade into the woodwork – or tile, if you want to get technical."

Kristi gave a delicate snort. "Tess, the last word that would even begin to describe you is 'inconspicuous. I doubt you could fade into anything.'" She mentally pictured the statuesque brunette with the Hawaiian features. With her dark caramel skin, warm black eyes, and magazine model figure, she never failed to turn male heads wherever she went.

"Yes, well, it's something that I'm going to have to work on." Her voice turned serious. "Honest. Are you all right? Where are you?"

Kristi hesitated. "I better not tell you that for your own safety. It's no secret that we're friends and I don't want to give you information that could get you hurt." She paused. "I'm not coming back to MiracleCorp."

"What…to work? Ever?"

"Ever."

"But…" Tess' protest was halfhearted. Kristi knew that

she too was having doubts about her work. It was a conversation they had had on numerous occasions.

"Tess. They're murderers. Or at least attempted murderers. They haven't actually killed anyone that we know about – yet. God has shown me in no uncertain terms that I am not to be a part of MiracleCorp anymore…and I really think you should think about leaving too. We can't keep justifying what we do. We may be doing good on the outside, but the inside is rotten to the core."

Kristi finished her words in a rush, praying she hadn't offended her friend. The silence on the other end wasn't encouraging.

"You know, Kristi," the words were drawn out as though Tess was thinking hard, "what you just said is basically confirmation of something I've been praying about for a while – as you well know. I've seen things that I didn't necessarily agree with – not that they were illegal, but just …immoral; unethical. I think God has been leading me – or rather us - to this point for a while now, don't you think?"

Kristi breathed a sigh of relief and a silent prayer of thanks. "Yes, I do. But pray about staying a little while longer. I think maybe God can use all of this to bring down MiracleCorp – although I think it's a real shame the company is corrupt. MiracleCorp has done some great things. And its CEO, James Sinclair, I truly believed he was a good man. Now to find out…" Kristi felt a sharp pang of regret slice through her.

"Yes, it's incredibly disappointing, but if it's rotten to the core, like it's appearing, then it needs to be exposed – especially if these people are so egocentric as to think they can go around trying to kill people and get away with it." Kristi could hear the outrage in Tess' normally mild voice.

Tess didn't know about her relationship to James Sinclair or most especially her relationship to Pamela Sinclair. As much as it pained her to think that the couple could be involved in the evil going on in the corporation, not even the fact that Pamela was her sister would stop Kristi from doing whatever it took to shut MiracleCorp's doors for good. She spoke into the phone. "My thoughts exactly. So, you'd be willing to help us out?"

"Just tell me what you need."

# # #

David leaned back in the chair and listened with unabashed interest to Kristi's side of the conversation. He still wasn't sure how he felt about Kristi's involvement with MiracleCorp, but right now he didn't know what to do about it.

She certainly seemed sincere – genuinely afraid for him and Grace. So why did he have an "itchy" feeling about her, like she was still hiding something from him?

The fact that she hadn't come clean with him right up front rankled. But, he argued with himself, she did give you that 'midnight' call to warn you to get away fast. And she sure is pretty. He watched her smooth features wrinkle in concentration as she listened to Tess. Her face was very expressive. She didn't hide what she thought very well – although she tried.

When Kristi said good-bye, David quickly steered his eyes back to Larry and Bob's antics. Grace was still engrossed in the duo. Kristi got up and walked over to sit beside him.

"Well?"

"Tess said she would do whatever we needed. I told her to start out by see what she could find on any secret testing done in a MiracleCorp lab. She's going to see if she can access the lab records now and will call us as soon as she knows anything." Kristi paused and David took the opportunity to jump in with a question.

"Do you think it'll be that easy?"

"Probably not." He liked the way she wrinkled her nose when she thought. "But, Tess is willing to hack into the computer system if necessary."

David smirked. "Is that ethical?"

Kristi's glare was hot enough to singe his raised eyebrows. He almost winced at the heat. "Is trying to kill you and your daughter and anyone who stands in the way of their goals ethical?" She spat the last word at him.

"Uh, no of course not." He gentled his tone. "I'm sorry. I guess I sound pretty ungrateful."

"Again."

Again? Oh, she was referring to the bed and breakfast conversation. "Uh, yeah, again. And again, I apologize."

Her expression softened a bit, but the heat in her eyes still blazed. "These guys made up the rules to this game, not me. And besides, she's only going to do that as a last resort."

David was in awe of this woman. She had more sides to her than a Rubik's Cube – and was just as hard to figure out. She was so gentle and sweet with Grace.

With him, she seemed to be mostly firecracker with a short fuse. When she was in "doctor mode" she was cool precision. Who was the real Kristi Henderson? David smiled to himself. Finding out might be the most fun he'd had in a long time.

Find someone to love her as much as I do. Lydia's voice rang so clear in his mind it was almost like she was standing beside him speaking aloud. His hands shook and he shoved them in his pockets to hide the tremors. David waited for the shaft of pain that normally lanced his heart at the memory of Lydia to come. When it didn't, he blinked.

"David?" Kristi's voiced jerked him back to the hotel room.

"Yeah?"

"Are you okay? You look a little pale." He felt her soft

hand on his cheek and saw that concern had replaced the fire in her eyes. He swallowed hard when he realized he wanted to kiss her. He spun away as quickly as he could manage without offending her and started picking up the paper that littered the table.

"Uh, yeah, sure. I'm fine. Something just reminded me of my wife." His eyes glanced back at her without his permission.

Her hand curled into a fist by her side. He wanted it back on his cheek. "Oh. I'm sorry."

"Hey, it's all right." He thought for a moment, then asked, "Did I do the right thing?"

Kristi frowned. "What do you mean?"

David shrugged and ran a hand through his hair again, doubts and fears plaguing him. "Running with Grace. Should I have just gone to the authorities?"

"I don't know, David. When I called you that night and told you to run, I truly believe that's what you were supposed to do. I had just read about escaping and running in the bible and when I got the call from Tess, I just knew that you were supposed run and I was supposed to help you."

"What about keeping Grace with us? Should I have sent her to Italy with my mother? Would she be safe right now if I had done that?" He just didn't know.

"David, Satan is the author of confusion. He wants you to doubt, to second guess yourself. Truthfully, I believe that the men would have followed Grace to Italy. They're not stupid. They're powerful and have the latest technology at their fingertips - not to mention some of the highest authority officials in their back pockets. They knew the moment your mother stepped on that plane - and they would have been right behind her if Grace had gone with her. So, no, I think you did the right thing."

David swallowed hard, grateful for the encouragement. She looked so earnest; obviously wanting to comfort him, help him quiet the turmoil that constantly raged through him.

"Daddy?"

David's attention immediately shifted to his daughter, grateful for the distraction from his attraction – and his confusion.

"What is it baby?"

"If I go with the men chasing us, will they leave you and Ms. Henderson alone?"

David's breath left his lungs with a whoosh and he ate the distance between Grace and him with two strides. He grabbed her up into his arms and buried his face in her curls. "No, sweetie, they wouldn't, so I don't want you even thinking that, okay?"

Unblinking blue eyes stared into his. She wasn't sure if she believed him – he could see it in the depths of her eyes.

Kristi's voice shook as she told him, "I'm going to catch a nap and give you two some time alone. Let me know if you want to walk over and get some dinner at the hotel restaurant."

David barely registered her words, but was thankful for her sensitivity to his need to be alone with his daughter. *God, what are you doing to my child?*

#

Kristi slipped into the adjoining room and shut the door. If only she could shut the door of her mind as easily. As weary as her body felt, her mind raced.

When would be a good time to tell David the rest of the truth? Tonight while they were eating? But what if he decided to tell her to get lost? He really would have trouble then. She had contacts that could help them that he couldn't even begin to imagine asking. A glance at the clock told her she had about an hour and a half to sleep. The restaurant opened at six for the evening meal. She was exhausted and starving.

But first – Kristi walked to the small overnight bag sitting in the chair beside the TV set and rummaged through it until she found what she was looking for.

She really needed to go to God before she took a nap. She needed to know what the next step in the plan was supposed to be, so the best place to go was to the blueprint. Curling her legs beneath her on the bed, she opened the bible in front of her and bowed her head. What do I read, Lord? What else do you have to tell me today?

As she often did with the word, Kristi flipped through several pages. Tell me when to stop, Lord. She turned a few more, then stopped. Jude? That gentle nudging of her spirit compelled her to read. The entire book was one chapter with twenty-five verses.

When she finished the book, she returned to the seventeenth verse, imprinting the words on her mind even as she read them aloud. "But you beloved, ought to remember the words that were spoken beforehand by the apostles of our Lord Jesus Christ, that they were saying to you, 'In the last time there shall be mockers following after their own ungodly lusts. These are the ones who cause divisions, worldly-minded, devoid of the spirit.' "

Kristi paused at this point. The people chasing us are worldly minded, and definitely not in your spirit. She read on picking back up at verse twenty.

"But you, beloved, building yourselves up on your most holy faith; praying in the Holy Spirit; keep yourselves in the love of God, waiting anxiously for the mercy of our Lord Jesus Christ to eternal life." Lord, are you saying we should prepare ourselves to die – soon?

Kristi finished the passage through verse twenty-three. "And have mercy on some, who are doubting; save others, snatching them out of the fire; and on some have mercy with fear, hating even the garment polluted by the flesh."

Okay, so some are doubting – I think that David would fit

in that category. He's definitely in need of your mercy. Save him Lord, save him before it's too late. I feel like he's a Christian, but he's just drifted from you in his grief and anger. So, who needs snatching from the fire? Show us what you want, where to go. Go in front of us and prepare the way.

Ignoring the grumbling of her stomach, she ordered her madly racing mind to halt, and stretched across the bed to give into slumber.

Ringing penetrated her consciousness. Without opening her eyes, she batted her hand in the general direction of the noise. When it didn't connect with anything, she forced an eyelid up. Consciousness returned with a vengeance as she realized where she was – and that the ringing sound was the phone.

She propelled her groggy body forward and grabbed the handset. "Hello?" It came out as a croak, but at least it came out.

"Kristi?"

"Yup."

"Uh, it's David. Did I wake you?"

"Yup."

Soft laughter filled her ear. "Are you sure?"

"Nope."

"Let me guess. You don't like to be waked up. You're one of those people that likes to wake up on their own."

"Yup."

His soft laughter became a full-fledged chuckle. "Are you hungry?"

"Uh huh." Her stomach chose that moment to register a complaint with its owner. She pried the other eye open. She had slept for an hour and a half. Better than nothing.

"Well, do whatever you've got to do to wake up and get out here. Grace and I are starving."

"Okay." She tossed the handset in the direction of the base and pulled the pillow over her head. When her stomach grumbled again, she sighed and sat up. Curls spilled over her eyes and she brushed them back as she spoke to her belly. "Okay, okay, I'm getting up. I'm going to feed you."

She was ready in ten minutes. It didn't take long to pull her hair up into a scrunchy while leaving some curls to twine around her ears. A good face and mouth scrub, along with a clean sweatshirt and pair of jeans and she felt like a new person.

Kristi spent a little more time on her make up all the while assuring herself it was not for David's benefit, but because it would make her feel more put together and confident in herself.

She met her gaze in the mirror and smirked. "Yeah, right."

When she stepped out of the room, David and Grace were perched in the two rockers located in front of their room. Two pairs of blue eyes looked up to smile at her appearance - and Kristi thought her heart would stop.

Oh my, she was falling in love. With the both of them.

#

Wow. David tried to force his brain to form a coherent thought. All he could see was a vibrant vision of loveliness when Kristi stepped out of her room. Thanks goodness Grace popped up out of her rocker to greet the woman, or he might have really embarrassed himself as he couldn't think of a single word to say to her.

"Ms. Kristi. You look beautiful. Smell good too." Okay, so he could have said that.

"You clean up pretty well." The words were no sooner out of his mouth that he wished he could recall them. You're an idiot, Walton. He needed to take lessons from a six year old on how to compliment a lady.

Kristi shot him a half grin, then focused her attention on Grace. At least he hadn't offended her. Instead, she laughed and said to Grace, "Thank you for noticing, dear lady." Kristi reached out a hand that Grace happily took. David wanted to hold Kristi's other hand, but contented himself with taking Grace's free one instead.

The picture of a happy family unit. He swallowed hard at the thought. Not once since Lydia's death had he even allowed himself to dream of one day loving another woman. David searched for something halfway intelligent to say.

"Hungry?" Oh, that was brilliant.

Kristi glanced his way and smiled. "Starved. What about you guys?"

"I want a hamburger and French fries." Grace quickly put in her order as she gave a little hop and grinned up at David.

He feigned shock. "But I think they're only serving liver and onions tonight. Isn't that what the menu said, Kristi?" He shot her a wink.

Kristi played along perfectly. "Oh yes, definitely, liver and onions with some broccoli on the side."

Grace pulled them to a screeching halt. She looked up, blue eyes wide, nose wrinkled with a totally disgusted expression on her impish face. "No way! I think I'm gonna barf."

David didn't have to feign shock this time. "Grace Walton. Where on earth did you hear that?"

Grace only looked a little guilty. "From Shelby Martinez in my Sunday School class." She pulled her hands away from Kristi and David and crossed her arms, the mutinous expression on her face a definite sign she was not eating liver and onions.

David heard Kristi try to smother a giggle. He shot her a look, but it was hard to keep a ferocious look on his face when he was trying so hard not to burst out laughing. What a relief to see that Grace was a normal little girl about some things. "So, that's what you're learning in Sunday School?"

Grace looked down and scuffed her shoe against the sidewalk. She mumbled, "Well, that's not the only thing."

"Uh, Grace?" Kristi spoke up and David and Grace turned their attention to her. "I don't like liver and onions either."

A beautiful smile beamed up at Kristi and David thought his heart would stop. How long had it been since he'd seen his little girl this relaxed and happy? What was it about Kristi that could make his little girl smile like that? He cleared his throat. "Okay, so what say we don't get the liver and onions and see if they have hamburgers and French fries with our names on them?"

"Yay, Daddy!"

"Yay, David!"

The two girls shot him grins of approval and David realized Kristi had thoroughly wormed her way into his heart in the span of a very short time.

#

A hamburger had never tasted so good to Kristi's deprived taste buds. When they had entered the hotel restaurant, the delicious smells had assaulted her senses and had her stomach growling warnings. Now, happily munching on the treat, Kristi watched the interaction between father and daughter. David was a good dad. Not perfect, but a good dad nevertheless.

He spoke, his deep voice breaking into her musings. "So, tell me a little about yourself."

Kristi munched a hot fry. "What do you want to know?"

"You know, where you grew up, did you get along with your parents, do you have any brothers and sisters. That kind of thing."

"I'll bore you to death. I had a relatively uneventful childhood."

"Try me."

Kristi took a deep breath. "Okay, I grew up in Greensburg, SC, but went to MUSC in Charleston to get my medical degree. I had just finished my residency when MiracleCorp recruited me."

"Why did you decide to become a doctor?"

Kristi smiled as she thought about that one. "My dad was a doctor, his dad was a doctor, and his dad was a doctor and so on." She gave a shrug. "I always knew I'd be a doctor."

"Did you ever think about doing anything else?"

"Nope."

David looked sincerely puzzled. "But, what if you'd hated it?"

Kristi smiled again. "I didn't so it wasn't an issue. I've always loved to help people. When I was old enough, I used to tag along to dad's practice on the days school was out and then during summer vacation. I did small things, observed him and others, and learned the ropes from the ground up, so to speak. I've just always loved the environment." She and her dad had had their problems, but when she was with him in his office, she felt like she belonged and he approved. "What about you?"

"Me?"

"Yeah, have you always wanted to be a carpenter?"

There was a slight hesitation before he answered her. "No, I wanted to fly planes for the Air Force."

"So what happened?"

He gave a slight shrug. "Bad eyes. They didn't have the kind of surgery back then like they do now. I used to wear glasses, but switched to extended wear contacts. Less of a pain."

"I want to be a doctor like Ms. Kristi." Grace's little voice piped into the conversation. Sometimes she was so quiet, Kristi could almost forget she was there.

David looked a little startled. "You do?"

"Uh huh. I like it when God let's me help heal people."

Kristi watched David quickly look around to see if any-one was listening, then saw him force a smile. "That's great, honey. Being a doctor is a very noble profession."

"Yeah, it's a good thing to do too."

This cracked them both up and the moment of tension was gone, but not forgotten. Grace looked a little confused as to why David and Kristi were laughing, but pleased that she'd been able to bring a smile to their faces.

"What about brothers and sisters?" David asked.

"One sister. I haven't seen her in a really long time. She left home years ago due to some stress between her and my parents, so I haven't talked to her in a while."

David's face suddenly sobered and fear darkened his gaze. Kristi was aware of it instantly. "David, what's wrong?"

His face was a pasty white. "They're here."

"Who?" Kristi asked although she felt sure she knew the answer.

"Don't make any sudden moves. The kitchen is behind us. When I say when, I want you to get up and move toward it. We'll go out that way and head to the car."

Kristi grabbed Grace's hand. The little girl trembled vio-lently, all traces of her former relaxation and feelings of security wiped away. She didn't say a word, just held Kristi's hand in a vice grip.

"Okay, go. Now. Hurry."

Kristi didn't even look behind her as she hurried toward the door, Grace in tow. She felt David's presence behind them.

"What about our things?"

"We'll get them. Most likely they checked our rooms and when we weren't there, came to find us. It's supper time after all. The restaurant would be the logical place to look. Hopefully, they're still looking and we can throw our things in the car."

The rooms weren't far and it was only a couple of minutes before they were throwing their things in their bags. Three minutes later, they were in the car and pulling out of the parking lot.

Once they were on the highway, David slapped a hand against the steering wheel.

Kristi jumped. "What was that for?"

"How do they keep finding us?"

Kristi thought if his jaw got any tighter, his teeth would shatter from the pressure. "I don't know. It can't be just dumb luck." She glanced back to check on Grace. The little girl was sitting stiff as a board. "It's okay sweetie, we're going to be fine."

"I'm scared." The little voice quivered. "They want me, don't they? I don't want them to take me away from my daddy – or you."

Kristi swallowed hard against the lump that suddenly formed in her throat. "I know and they're not going to. Hey, do know the song about the bible verse?"

Grace shook her head. "No, what is it?"

Kristi started to sing, trying to keep the quiver out of her voice. "When I am afraid, I will trust in Him, I will trust in Him. When I am afraid, I will trust in Him. The Lord who loves me so. Do you think you can sing it with me?"

Grace nodded and they began to sing together, both taking comfort in the fact that God was taking care of them. Kristi stopped singing mid-verse. Grace stopped too and asked, "What's wrong, Ms. Kristi?"

"The money."

David glanced over at her. "What?"

She spied the briefcase on the seat beside Grace. "It's the money. I bet they've got some sort of tracking device in there." Her eyes flew to David's. "I'm going to see if I can find it." Without waiting for a response, she scrambled over into the spacious backseat and grabbed the case. Her thumbs flicked the latches and the lid lifted easily.

A whistle blew out between her teeth as she took in the sight of the stacks of rubber-banded bills. "Wow."

"Yeah, it's a lot of money."

"No kidding. Okay, focus Henderson." She ran her fingers along the lining of the top. Nothing. Stacking the bills beside her, she emptied the briefcase and felt along the bottom and sides. A small lump in the back left corner gave her pause.

"I think I found it." She reached up to the armrest in the middle of the two front seats and opened the storage compartment. "Can you hand me that pocket knife in there?"

David's right hand reached in and pulled out the knife. "Here."

"Thanks." Kristi opened the blade and began cutting around the lining. When she had enough cut, she pulled it away and stuck her fingers into the opening.

"Got it." She pulled out a small round metallic device. "Want me to toss it out the window?"

"No, hold on to it for a few minutes."

Kristi raised an eyebrow, but didn't say anything. When David pulled off the highway onto an exit ramp, Kristi shot him a 'what are you doing?' look, but continued to hold her tongue. David drove for another five minutes before exclaiming, "Ah ha. Just what I was looking for."

A tractor trailer idled in the parking lot of the truck stop. Kristi watched David palm the little tracking device. "Are you going to do what I think you're going to do?"

"Yeah, Daddy, what are you going to do?"

He shot Kristi a satisfied grin. "What is it you think I'm going to do?"

Kristi couldn't help herself. She grinned back. "Exactly what it looks like you're going to do."

"Yup, that's what I'm doing."

"So do it and let's get out of here."

"Consider it done."

Kristi groaned and rolled her eyes, amazed they could find something to laugh at within the tenseness of their situation. "David..."

"All right, all right. Be right back, I gotta buy some tape." He climbed out of the Suburban and approached the all night store/diner.

Kristi watched him go. She could get used to sparring with him on a daily basis. *What do you think, God? Can something good come out of a big mistake on my part? I'd really appreciate it if you would work all things for the good of those who love you.*

The clamoring ring of the cell phone made Kristi jump and jerk her arm into the dash. "Ouch!"

"You okay, Ms. Kristi?"

Kristi mumbled, "Yes," as she dug into her purse. She found it on the fourth ring. "Hello?"

"Kristi?"

"Tess!"

"Hey, are you guys all right?"

"Yes, so far. We found a tracking device hidden in this suitcase of money they gave David to buy his cooperation."

Kristi heard Tess suck in a sharp breath. "These guys play nasty, don't they?"

"Yes, indeed they do. So, have you got anything?"

"That's why I'm calling."

"So soon?"

"I made an excuse to slip out the house and go to the office for a couple of hours. You'll never guess what I found."

"What?" Kristi could hardly breathe her anticipation was so great.

"There's a family in Oklahoma. From a little town called Clebit."

"Clebit? What's a Clebit?"

Kristi heard Tess giggle in spite of the seriousness of the

topic. "It's a little town in Okalahoma. There was a sixteen-year-old son who was supposed to have the spiritual gift of healing. He was here for a week, then he disappeared."

"What do you mean disappeared?"

"Just that. There's no record of why he was here, any testing done on him – at least none that I can find – or any documentation other than his name in the computer – with the notation 'healer' out beside it and the dates he was here. I'm wondering if someone just did a sloppy job of erasing his files and I just got lucky by stumbling on this little piece of information."

"Luck probably didn't have a lot to do with it."

"That's true. God is awesome, isn't He?"

"He is and if He wanted me to have this information, it's for a good reason. Okay, do you have an address on this family?"

"I sure do. Directions how to get there, too."

Kristi scrambled for a pen.

Chapter 8

James stopped mid-stride when he heard his wife's voice come from the room to his left. He had his foot on the first step, headed upstairs to visit with Seth for a few moments before going into the office. Pamela was in the den talking with Geoff. He couldn't seem to help himself. His feet carried him to stand outside the doorway to listen.

"Who is she, Geoff?" Pamela had her back to him, facing the fireplace where Geoff stood poking the dying embers. Neither could see him from where they stood, but he had a perfect view of the two figures.

Geoff gave the wood one more jab before glancing up at Pamela. "Just someone I work with. A nice girl. You'd like her."

"Really?"

"Yes, really. Why the sudden interest?"

"You know I care for you, Geoff. I always have and I always will." She walked over to rest a fine boned hand on his shoulder. James wilted at the sight.

Geoff shrugged her off. "You made your choice a long time ago. A lot of choices that I had no say in if I recall correctly."

Pamela's features stiffened at the accusation. "Yes, I did make my choice...choices. And choosing James is probably the only choice I don't regret for a minute. But that doesn't mean that I can just turn off caring about you. I want to see you happy." James was glad to hear she didn't regret marrying him. Glad she was willing to share that fact with Geoff.

Geoff turned cold, hard eyes in her direction and James winced at the sight, but continued to maintain his silence. When Geoff spoke, his tone matched his eyes. "You saw me happy about sixteen years ago, if I recall correctly."

Pamela threw her hands up, clearly exasperated with the younger man. "Can you not let it go? Does it still eat at you that much? We were teenagers, for goodness sake! Sixteen years old, Geoff. Mere children. Stop obsessing on it."

Geoff stepped swiftly toward her and for a moment James thought he was going to hit her. James started to move forward, but Geoff stopped and swung away and James slipped back unseen. Geoff's hands gripped the mantle and he spoke to the fire. "Yes, it still eats at me that much – sometimes. And we may have been young, but I know what I felt." He shrugged. "Anyway, like I said, I've met someone new. Maybe she can make me happy. Time will tell."

Pamela said, "You're still a young man – a handsome man. You deserve to marry and have children – to be happy."

Geoff barked out a harsh laugh. "Well, you're right about one thing. I do deserve children. However, fine lot of good that's done my brother hasn't it? How much happiness has he seen these last years – especially since Seth's diagnosis?"

James choked back his own gasp, but even if he hadn't, Pamela's sharply inhaled breath would have covered any sound he made. Tears pooled in her eyes and her features paled noticeably. "I can't believe you said that."

Geoff heaved a sigh. "I can't either. I'm tired and not totally aware of what I'm saying. So...I'll say goodnight."

James stepped into the room, acting as though he had just arrived. "Hello, you two. What's going on?"

Pamela swallowed nervously and Geoff looked back at the fire. James decided to let them off the hook. He turned to Pamela. "How's Seth?"

"The same," she whispered.

"Well, at least he's not worse."

"No, not yet."

James walked over and took her hand. "Geoff, have you found our miracle yet?"

"I've found her. I've just got to get her."

"How hard can it be, man? Just ask her parents to let her come see Seth. She can do her thing and be gone within the hour."

"It's not that simple, James. Her mother is dead and her father is very protective. He's not letting anyone get close to her. In fact, he's running with her and we don't have any idea where they are at this moment."

James could feel his frustration mounting with each word that came out of Geoff's mouth. "So, you've found the one person that could possibly help Seth and you can't get to her? You know I don't care how much it costs. Get that girl here. All of your other 'miracles' have turned up void – or dead. This one seems to be the real McCoy. I want her here within a week. You got it?"

Geoff's jaw was tight, but James didn't care. He'd do whatever he had to do to save his son.

"Got it." Geoff ground between clenched teeth as he stalked by, brushing off Pamela's attempt to sooth him with a hand on his arm.

James hated the rift he was causing between himself and his brother, but this was his son's life he was trying to save and if he had to sacrifice his brother to do it – then so be it.

"You really shouldn't antagonize him like that." Pamela's weary admonishment didn't help James' volatile emotions right now.

"And you should probably stay away from him. It does no good to stir up the past."

Pamela crossed to his side and placed a hand on his

rough, unshaven cheek, as she looked into his eyes. "James, you know you're the one I love. Yes, I can't help but care about Geoff, but I chose you and I chose Seth."

"Yes, you did. Unfortunately, it looks like you may have made the wrong choices - the wrong husband, the wrong child..." James stopped. He let his thumb brush across Pamela's cheek and wipe away the tears trickling down. "I'm sorry. I'm not worth much these days. I need to get out of here." He headed for the door. "I'll be back in time for supper."

It was Sunday afternoon. He headed for his office.

#

While Kristi and Grace waited in the car, David made his way to the cash register, duct tape in hand. Cigarette smoke burned his lungs and made his eyes water.

CNN silently played in one corner of the little convenience store. The volume was probably turned down because it wouldn't do any good to try to hear over the noise in the place. Truckers laughed and joked and blew off steam after a long day on the road.

David stood in line for a brief minute before realizing that the spot between his shoulder blades itched. He turned casually to scan the area behind him. Beards and tattoos; clean-shaven and businesslike. The place held a mixture of cultures.

Along with a lone woman watching him with speculative brown eyes. David gave her a nod and a polite smile before turning back to the counter. Who was she? Did he know her? He glanced back. She was gone.

"Sir?"

David jerked back to the counter. It was his turn and the cashier did nothing to hide her impatience. Long red fingernails tapped the counter in a jerky rhythm that kept time with the gum snapping between the woman's teeth.

"Oh, sorry. Here." He tossed the tape on the counter and pulled out a twenty-dollar bill.

Gum popped. "That'll be seven twenty-nine."

Highway robbery. David held his tongue and handed over the money. He watched the news while waiting for the woman to make the change. When a picture of Grace popped up on the screen, his heart just about hit the soles of his feet. His eyes grabbed at the closed captioned words running across the bottom of the screen.

"David Walton and his six year old daughter, Grace, disappeared from their home early yesterday afternoon. Nancy Walton, David Walton's mother is also missing. The home was apparently broken into sometime Saturday night or early Sunday morning. Neighbors reported suspicious activity to local authorities who found the home ransacked when they arrived to investigate. If anyone has any information on the whereabouts of this family or the break in, concerned friends and family have set up a special number to call. It is posted at the bottom of your screen – or you can call your local police station with any information." The report concluded with pictures of himself and his mother in the upper right hand corner of the screen. Nothing had been said about Grace and her healings. How odd. Although, he supposed he should be thankful for it.

David swallowed hard, wishing he had thought to wear some type of disguise. Any minute now he expected someone to tackle him to the floor. Who were these supposedly friends and family with the special number? He bet that number went straight to MiracleCorp headquarters.

"Hey!" The disgruntled cashier waved his change in his face.

"Oh, sorry."

"Good grief, man, wake up." She slapped the change in his outstretched hand. "Have a nice day."

"Right." David pocketed the change, grabbed his brown bag with the tape and headed for the door. He kept his head ducked low and wished he'd thought to buy a baseball cap and sunglasses.

No more than two steps out the double glass doors and he felt a hand on his arm. David's legs froze his forward motion, while his heart tripped into overdrive.

"Excuse me, sir?" The soft voice calmed his racing pulse only slightly. He turned to see the woman who had been staring at him earlier while he had been standing in line.

"Yes?" David willed himself to stay calm; normal – if there was such a thing anymore. A pair of weary gray eyes stared up into his. This woman meant him no harm. His knees felt weak, but he forced himself to stay upright. "Can I help you?"

Her eyes shifted to the right, then back. "My name's Mary. I...um... I recognize you from the television. I was also at the healing service when your wife died two years ago. I'm so sorry for your loss."

David swallowed hard. "Thank you, Mary." Where was she heading with this?

"I've also heard about what your daughter can do. Healing all those people in the doctor's office and such."

Mary went right where he thought she was going. David sighed. No point in denying it. "Yes, it's been pretty incredible – and scary - in more ways than one."

The woman's lank brown hair and gray eyes were nothing that would stand out in a crowd. But the determination stamped on her features made David take another look. She was dressed warmly, if cheaply. Her shoes looked like they had seen a few miles. Mary's voice brought his gaze back to hers. "We follow the circuit. You know, go where the healing services go."

"We?"

"My husband and daughter. We have nine year old beautiful girl." Pride made her face glow. But there was sadness there also.

David shifted his weight and glanced toward the car. Grace was staring out the window grinning at him. He gave her a little wave and turned back to excuse himself. The silent tears running down Mary's face startled him so bad he almost dropped his bag.

"Ma'am? Are you all right?"

She sniffed and searched her pockets for a tissue. "No, no, I'm not all right. My daughter's blind. She was in a car accident three years ago and hasn't been able to see since." The words exploded from her lips and David stepped back.

"Hey, look, I'm sorry for you, but I've got to go." Fear was now a living thing, coursing swiftly through his veins. He knew what she was going to ask and he didn't even want to go there.

"Please...," she beseeched him.

When David felt the small hand slip into his, he knew he was defeated. Looking down into Grace's impish little face made him realize he really had no choice.

"Please, Daddy?"

David hung his head and closed his eyes. When are you going to accept what God can do through your daughter?

Right now David almost wished he didn't believe in God.

But, he did.

"Sure, Grace. You can help her." And God, could you please protect her? Us? How much time do we have before those guys catch up with us anyway? He couldn't believe he was actually praying to the God he had sworn never to speak to again.

David looked back up at Mary. "Where's your daughter?"

Joy lit her eyes and she grabbed his arm to pull him along behind her. David pulled Grace and the three of them made their way over to the cab of a truck. Mary pulled open the door.

"Janet? Janet, honey? You awake?"

"Yeah, I'm awake." A small boned girl with her mother's features was lying on the front seat. She sat up when she felt her mother touch her jean-clad leg.

"Hey, I've brought someone to see you."

"Lucky them." Her tone was sullen; sightless eyes stared at nothing. David felt his heart go out to this young girl.

"Janet, you be polite. They're here to help you."

David reached out to touch the girl. "Do you believe God can heal you?"

"Sure, but why would he want to when he made me this way in the first place?" The tone was still sullen, the question cynical.

David glanced over at Mary who stood chewing on an already decimated fingernail. She shrugged. David took a deep breath and dug into his tired mind for an answer. All those years in church had to be worth something. "Look kid, God didn't make you this way. He doesn't make bad things happen; that's the devil's job. It's an imperfect world and God just wants to love you – and for you to love him."

Again, David felt a hand slip into his. Only this time, he knew it wasn't Grace's. It was small, but not small enough. He looked over to see Kristi smiling at him. Tears shimmered in her green eyes.

"Did you just hear what you said?"

David blinked and mentally ran through his words, then he leaned over to whisper in her ear, "Yeah, I guess I did. But that doesn't mean I believe it."

"Yes, you do," she whispered back. David hated it when she was right.

"Hey Mom! I can see you! Where's Dad? Get Dad!" The shout had David and Kristi whipping around to see Grace laughing and jumping up and down, clapping her hands; her ringlets dancing on her shoulders in time with her feet.

Mother and daughter were embracing, tears streaming down both of their faces.

"We missed it." David stared at the girl's eyes that now took in everything they could focus on. "Grace, what'd you do?"

Grace shrugged and grinned again. "I just asked God if he'd take away the darkness. And he did."

Janet ran up to Grace and grabbed her in a big bear hug. "Thank you. Thank you!"

"Don't thank me, thank God."

"David." Kristi's tug on his shirt distracted him.

"Yeah?"

"Look."

A dark black sedan pulled slowly into the parking lot.

# # #

"Do you think they realize they're chasing a decoy?" Instead of the eighteen-wheeler, David had managed to slip the tracking device onto one of the Harley's parked at one of the gas stations. The owner obviously wasn't staying long, thus the reason he was chosen to be the host for the device.

Mary and Janet had created a diversion for Kristi, David and Grace and the trio had managed to drive away undetected.

David gave a grim smile. "Let's hope not. At least not for the next few hours. If I don't get a good night's sleep, I'm not going to be worth squat."

Kristi yawned, then laughed when Grace did the same. "I know what you mean. Let's start looking for a place to sleep. I think it's safe to use this credit card again."

David nodded, obviously not liking the idea of using Kristi's money, but clearly understanding it was the only option for right now.

He swung back on I-40 west heading for Okalahoma and a little town called Clebit.

"I know it's getting late, but what do you say we put some distance between those two goons and us. I'll drive for a couple of hours and then we can find us a hotel."

Kristi nodded. "I'd feel better if we were further away from them. At least we now know how they kept finding us."

"Daddy, I'm tired of riding. I wanna go home."

Kristi turned to see the tired little girl sitting with her arms around her favorite stuffed toy. An oversized VeggiTale character named Larry. This was the first time she'd heard Grace complain. Frankly she was surprised it had taken her this long to say something.

David's voice came from beside Kristi's left. "Grace, I know it's been a long couple of days, but we can't go home just yet. I'm going to find a way to make sure you're safe. There are bad men out there that want to take you away from me and I'm not going to let that happen."

Kristi winced, wondering if he should be so blunt with the child. Grace was quiet for a moment, then she spoke softly. "And you can't keep me safe at home?"

"No baby, unfortunately, I can't."

"Then I guess it's okay. I'll try to be patient."

David smiled in the rearview mirror, but Kristi saw the pain in his eyes. "That's my girl."

Grace fell silent, lost in her little girl thoughts.

Guilt and self-recriminations rose quickly to the surface. Kristi wanted to comfort David, but knew that if she hadn't started the hunt for Grace in the first place, the father and daughter would be safe and happy at home.

She reached over to rest a hand on his arm and gave a slight squeeze. His left hand covered hers and squeezed back. The slight sheen in his eyes brought tears to her own. She quickly looked out the window and blinked rapidly.

She had to find a way to tell him everything. He would forgive her. He had to, because if he didn't, Kristi didn't know how she would go about waking up each morning for the rest of her life.She heard him clear his throat.

"So, tell me how you became such a believer in Christ."

Kristi blinked at the question from left field. "You know, you really have a habit of doing that to me."

David looked startled for a moment as he shot her a brief glance before turning his attention back to the highway. "What do you mean by that?"

"You just come up with these questions. It's like playing Russian roulette. You never know if the next question you ask is going to be loaded or not."

David burst into laughter. "And you have quite a habit of doing that to me."

"What?" Kristi was genuinely bewildered by his mirth.

David sobered and shot her a look that spoke volumes. "Making me laugh just when I think that there's nothing left to laugh about. Thank you." He reached out with his right hand to pick up her left. When he pressed a soft kiss to the back of it, Kristi's heart didn't whether to speed up or slow down.

She gulped. "Uh, well, you're welcome – I think."

"No, it's definitely a good thing." He smiled her way again and kept his hold on her hand. It was a good thing she was sitting down as her legs had turned to jell-o.

"So?"

"So what?" Kristi parried.

David looked at her out of the corner of his eye and didn't say anything else. Kristi knew what he was waiting for. "Okay, my background. You want the full length novel or the Reader's Digest version."

"The full length novel."

"Right. Somehow, I knew you were going to say that."

"Quit stalling."

Kristi gave a little laugh and began. "Well, I was born twenty eight years ago, on Christmas Day, to a couple named…"

"If you say 'Mom and Dad', I'm going to tickle you."

As delightful as that sounded, Kristi thought it safer not to test him while he was driving.

"As I was saying – named, Arthur and Julie Henderson."

"My mommy's name was Lydia."

The warmth of the moment was shattered when David jerked at Grace's voice. His hand slipped away from hers and found its way back to the steering wheel. Kristi's hand felt cold and she curled her fingers into a ball. Her hand missed his. Was that possible?

She cleared her throat. "I know, honey. That's a beautiful name. I'm sure you miss her very much."

"Sometimes. Not as much as I used to. Sometimes I can't remember what she looks like until I see her picture." Grace's voice didn't hold much emotion. She didn't sound sad; more like she was just stating a fact.

Kristi stole a look at David. He was staring straight ahead, but there wasn't any tension in his face. Kristi raised an eyebrow. Interesting. God, is he letting you heal him?

"Let Kristi finish her story, Grace. Okay?"

"Okay Daddy." Grace settled back into her seat and pulled a book out of her backpack.

David smiled at her, but didn't reach to take her hand again. "Go ahead."

"You're sure you want to hear this?"

"Quite."

"Okay, anyway. I grew up in a pretty good home, I guess. I had very strict parents. They taught good values, morals, etc., but never went to church or heard much about God. I mean I knew He was out there, but I never really gave Him much thought, you know?"

David nodded and Kristi continued. "Then one day, Tess came to work at MiracleCorp."

"Ah yes, the friend and co-worker."

Kristi tried to read a hidden meaning in that statement,

but couldn't find one. She ignored it and went on. "Yes, my friend and co-worker. You have to know Tess to understand her. Not only is she absolutely brilliant, she's absolutely gorgeous. When she came to work, she was very intimidating to a lot of people – including myself, although I hate to admit it. And then one day, about three months after she started working there, I found her crying in the bathroom."

"Crying?"

"Yeah. I didn't know whether to ignore her and leave her alone, or ask her what was wrong."

"You asked her what was wrong." David made the statement with total certainty in his voice. Kristi smiled at him. He was getting to know her well.

"Of course I did."

"Of course."

"You know what she said? She said she was lonely. She said she had been praying and praying for God to send her a friend, and she was still waiting for an answer. I must have had a funny look on my face because she asked me if I believed in prayer."

"What'd you say?"

"I told her I guess I did, that I hadn't really thought about it one way or another. That led to her talking about God and how wonderful He was. I think I said something like if he was so wonderful why was she sitting in the bathroom crying her eyes out?"

"Good question."

"I thought so. But she had an even better answer."

"I figured she might."

"She stopped for a minute and just looked at me. Then she gave me this beautiful smile and said, 'So you could find me.'"

"Wow."

"Yeah. We had lunch everyday after that and she talked me into going to church with her and getting involved with a singles group there. One night the pastor gave an invitation and I knew it was time. God had been working on my heart and by the time the invitation came that night, I was ready for it. That was a little over two years ago."

"Two years ago, I buried my wife and decided that God didn't want anything to do with me – so I didn't want anything to do with Him." Kristi listened silently, her heart aching for the loss she heard in his voice.

"Do you still believe that?"

He didn't answer her question right away. In fact he was silent for so long, she wondered if he was going to answer. Finally, the words came, although they sounded grudging, as though he really didn't want to say them, but couldn't seem to help it. "No. I don't suppose I really do. I mean, I sure don't understand why He took Lydia from us when He did or why He's allowed Grace to have the kind of gift she's got, but He has. Maybe, I just have to accept that I won't ever have an answer and move on. I don't know."

"At least He's kept us safe so far."

David smiled over at her. "Yes, He has done that, hasn't He?"

It was a start.

Chapter 9

James' fist pounded the desk. He was working from home again today. "Where is she? It's Monday morning. I thought you were going to have her here last night."

He was trying to keep his cool, but he knew that two veins stood out on his forehead. Pamela always commented on them when he lost his temper. And his temper was definitely lost. Fear, unfamiliar, and unwelcome, churned in his gut and that simply added fuel to the fire. Seth had not had a good night. Pamela was reaching the point of giving up hope.

Geoff defended himself. "Look James. I'm doing the best I can do. I mean, I've got the best guys on it. They lost them somewhere. Apparently they found the tracking device that was in the money I used to buy off the dad. They got smart and stuck it on a motorcycle. When my guys caught up with him, they realized what happened. However, they do seem to be heading west on I-40 for some reason. We'll keep going the same direction and hope we can catch up." Geoff paced back and forth, rubbing his knuckles across his chin.

"Hope?" James snapped. "Hope's not going to do it. Find a way to catch up to them and do it. Use the helicopter if necessary."

"James?"

The sound of his wife's voice brought his head around.

Grief and worry had left their mark, but they hadn't erased any of her natural beauty. He'd fallen in love with her the first time he'd seen her seventeen years ago. "What is it, my dear?"

"Seth's awake and asking to see you."

"I'll be right there." James watched Pamela leave the room. He turned back to his brother and was shocked at the anguish on the younger man's features.

"Geoff, are you all right?" Geoff's face smoothed immediately and James almost wondered if he was seeing things.

Geoff sighed raked a hand through his immaculately groomed hair. Then realizing what he'd done, he cursed and smoothed it back into place. "Of course. Look, I have to go. I'm meeting Teresa for lunch in an hour." He began heading for the door.

"Teresa? Your new girlfriend?"

"Yeah, she's great. You'd like her."

"Bring her by sometime, we'd love to meet her." James was curious about the woman who had captured Geoff's attention. She had to be someone special. After all Geoff claimed he was married to his work.

"You know James, sooner or later, I'm going to have to return to the lab. People are going to be suspicious that I'm out so much. First keeping an eye on the kid and working with that Henderson woman; now I'm chasing them all over the country. This is taking up quite a bit of time."

"Find the Walton girl and you can get back to your precious slides." James snarled, his temper back into full force. "This is my son's life we're talking about."

"Well, James, I hate to be the one to break it to you, but sometimes people die and there's not a blessed thing you can do about it. Maybe you just need to accept that fact." Geoff's own temper was obviously rising quickly, but James had to let him know in no uncertain terms that he would never give up on Seth.

"Never." This time his voice was soft. Lethal.

Geoff just stared at him for a moment before shoving the door open and leaving without another word. He slammed it behind him.

James sat, breathing hard. Never would he give up. Never would he accept that his son would die. There was a little girl out there in the world that could heal his son. He'd find her, and he'd find her soon.

James pushed away from his desk and headed upstairs to visit with his son. He wanted to tell him again of the miracle that was coming his way.

# # #

It had been a rough night. One filled with bad dreams; people chasing and shooting at them – and stealing Grace right out from under his nose. David groaned and scrubbed his sleep weary face. He hauled himself into the small bathroom and studied his face in the mirror above the sink. You're getting bags under your eyes, Walton.

At least he could stop worrying about his mother. She had called from Italy to let him know she had arrived safely. No doubt chatting a mile a minute with her sister. Distance had not diminished the closeness of those two. He finished shaving and brushing his teeth.

David walked over and looked down at his sleeping child. Grace was still snoring softly. So innocent. So sweet. He leaned down and placed a soft kiss on her cheek. What would he do without her? Just the thought sent terror shooting through his heart. How would he protect her?

You can't fully protect her. Only God can do that.

Where had that thought come from? Turning her over to God was not an option right now. He had turned Lydia over to God and she had died. Tears of helplessness welled up in his eyes. He just didn't know what to do. God, why is this happening? I don't understand. Haven't we been through enough? If I trust you with my child will you take her away from me?

The knock on the door startled him and he hurried to finish throwing on his clothes. He wiped his eyes and glanced at the clock. He was running late. They were supposed to be on the road in ten minutes.

David opened the door to Kristi's sweet face. Her beauty always stunned him. Her face was shining, devoid of makeup and her curls were pulled up into a ponytail with little wispy hairs curling at her temples. Her blue jeans and lightweight jacket made her look like she should be roaming the halls of the local high school. He took a deep breath. "Good morning, gorgeous."

Her right eyebrow lifted at the endearment, but the flush that swept through her cheeks told him she liked it.

"Good morning to you too. Are you ready?"

"Almost. I've got to wake Grace up. She's a sleepyhead this morning."

"I'll wake her. You can go ahead and get our bags in the car if you like."

David smiled his thanks. "Sure. That'd be great."

Kristi crossed over to the double bed where his daughter lay stretched out in peaceful slumber. Kristi paused and looked back at him. "It seems almost a crime to interrupt that good sleep."

David laughed. "Tell me about it. That's why she's still snoozing away. I didn't have the heart to wake her."

"You want to wait until she wakes up on her own?"

David shrugged. "I don't know. Are we in a hurry? We can make it to Clebit, Oklahoma in about six hours. We made good time last night."

Instead of stopping as planned, they had kept driving into the wee hours of the morning, talking and sharing. Neither had wanted the time to end. They finally stopped in the town of Memphis, Tennessee when David could no longer keep his eyes open. Kristi had dropped into a light doze about an hour earlier, her head resting uncomfortably against the window.

She smiled at him. "Okay, why don't we sit outside on the bench. We can leave the door cracked. It's chilly, but not too cold."

"Sure. Let me grab some shoes and tuck the blankets around Grace a little more."

David shoved his feet into the only pair of shoes he had brought. An old pair of brown loafers. At least they were comfortable.

After snuggling Grace into the covers to keep the draft off of her, he stepped outside to see Kristi sitting on an old bench opposite the room. He had a good view of the door and they could talk above a whisper and not wake up Grace.

"How'd you sleep?" David asked the first thing that came to mind. He was unimpressed with his brilliance. Kristi didn't seem to mind though, as she tossed him another smile.

"I slept all right. I don't think I'll really be able to sleep deep until all of this is over. I'm ready to get to Clebit and talk to this Dunn family." She picked up a dry, brown leaf off the seat beside her and it crumbled in her hand.

David watched the brittle pieces scatter in the wind and decided that could have symbolized his heart last week. It had looked whole on the outside, but if you touched it too hard, it would have crumbled into little pieces. He didn't feel like that so much now. And that had a lot to do with the woman sitting beside him.

He smiled at the thought.

"What?"

Kristi brought him out of his philosophical musings. "What?"

"No, that was my question. You smiled. At what?"

"My thoughts. Sometimes I crack myself up."

"Wanna share?"

Did he want to share? He looked at the door to the hotel room. It was still cracked and Grace was still sleeping. He missed sharing his thoughts with a woman; a partner – a wife. What would Lydia think about Kristi?

David didn't even hesitate with that one. "Lydia would have liked you." The words seemed to pop from his tongue of their own volition.

Kristi didn't look surprised; she just raised an eyebrow. "You think?"

"Yes, I think. I know I like you."

Her eyes flitted from his for a brief moment and David wondered at the cause. He still felt she was hiding something, but didn't think it was anything that would cause him or Grace harm. He really believed she was coming to care for them. She showed it in everything she did. After all, she saved their lives.

"David, I need to talk to you about…"

"Daddy?"

His sleepy child stood in the doorway. It was time to get on the road. He looked over at Kristi and held out a hand. "Ready?"

She hesitated briefly, then took hold of his hand. "Sure. Let's go."

David decided he could get used to the feel of her hand in his. He didn't let go until he had to help Grace get dressed.

# # #

Kristi found herself looking forward to the drive. Her hand still tingled where David had held it. She felt like a teenager again with her first crush. Only this was on a deeper level. Sure, she was attracted to him – he was gorgeous, what's not to be attracted to?

But it was much more than his blue eyes and dimples. He was nice. He cared. He was an outstanding father. And he was coming back to his faith. God was once again becoming a focal point in his life. A priority.

Kristi only prayed that once he found out who she was and what her role in this drama was, however unintentional, that he wouldn't throw it all away. Please God, don't let him turn his back on you again. And give me the words to say to him.

She tossed the hotel key on the bed. The convenience of speedy checkout. Just leave the key in the room and we'll charge your card. And speaking of charging the card, it was probably getting close to the max. Not only that, did they dare continue to use it? David had had close to a hundred dollars in cash in his wallet when they left. She wasn't sure, but it had to be a lot less than that by now. She knew she had about fifty in cash.

Kristi sighed and grabbed her purse. David already had her bag stashed in the car; she had just wanted one last look around to make sure she had everything. Not that she had that much to keep up with, but old habits died hard.

"Ready?" David stood in the door, holding it open for her.

"Yes, I think so. If I've forgotten anything, I sure can't think of what it might be."

"Come on and we'll get some breakfast on the road. We should be there by two o'clock or so."

"Okay, I'm anxious to find out what a Clebit is. A town so small the population isn't even listed has to be something to see."

David laughed. "Just don't blink or you'll miss it."

Six and a half hours later, Grace was cranky, David was exhausted and Kristi's nerves had just about had it. Three bathroom breaks and a thirty-minute stop for lunch had everyone on edge. Frankly Kristi wouldn't mind letting loose with a good Tarzan yell.

But there was the house. In the middle of Clebit, Oklahoma.

The town was exactly what she'd expected. One main street, and a few scattered houses off little side streets. A small grocery store, a post office from the 1800's, and a mom and pop restaurant were all within walking distance of the little house on the corner of Edwards Creek Road.

"That's it." David's voice broke the silence.

"So, what do we do? Just go knock on the door? You think anyone's home?"

David began climbing out of the car. "Only one way to find out. Come on Grace, you need to stretch your legs anyway."

Grace couldn't move fast enough to get out of the car. Kristi followed more slowly, working the kinks out of her cramped joints. She didn't ride well and the last couple of days were taking their toll, not only on her body, but her nerves. She winged a prayer for patience and followed the father and daughter up to the weary looking front porch.

There was no doorbell, so David knocked on the door that desperately needed a paint job. A brief shuffle could be heard from inside, then the door opened a small crack. Kristi placed the woman in her late thirties.

"Yes? I don't have any money if you're selling anything."

David spoke. "No ma'am. We're here to talk to you about a company named MiracleCorp."

The slamming of the door rang loudly in their ears. Kristi raised an eyebrow. "Guess we've got the right house."

"I'd say so." David knocked again, then hollered. "Ma'am, please. We're not here to harm you. We just need some questions answered."

No response.

Kristi decided to try. "Mrs. Dunn, some men who work for MiracleCorp are after David's little girl. We know your son died while in their care and we want to know what happened and how to keep David's daughter safe. Please, can you help us?"

The door cracked again. "I've told you people I wouldn't say nothing about nothing. I thought you were gonna leave me be." The twang of the west rang in the woman's voice. Kristi immediately thought of Reba McEntire, the country western singer.

"We're not here representing MiracleCorp. We're running from them." David must have decided to just lay it on the line. Apparently this tactic worked for the door opened another two inches. Mud brown eyes stared back at them.

"Well, come on in then. I reckon you can sit a spell and tell me what the dickens is going on now."

Kristi immediately noticed the odor of illness when she stepped inside. She wrinkled her nose and tried to ignore it. Grace didn't bother to hide her disgust.

"Ew. It stinks in here."

"Grace!" David's mortification came through loud and clear. The woman didn't seem to be bothered and her whole one hundred pounds quivered as she gave a small laugh. "Yes, it does. My boy is having a hard time right now. He's laid up sick in the other room. He's battling Leukemia."

Grace looked contrite. "I'm sorry. I didn't mean to hurt your feelings. Sometimes I say things I should keep in my brain. I didn't mean to say that out loud."

"It's quite all right child. It's the truth. It does stink in here. I reckon I've gotten used to it. Why don't you go in and visit with him. He don't get much company. Now," she turned to David and Kristi and motioned for them to sit on the beat up couch that was against the far wall, "how do you know my name and my connection with MiracleCorp and what do you think I can do to help you?"

"You had another son, didn't you?" Kristi asked quietly. David took a seat beside her on the couch.

Mrs. Dunn pushed her limp brown hair back from her forehead. "Yeah, I did. Billy died last year."

"What happened?"

"Don't rightly know. He was fine when we went to the healin' service for Dwayne. Then two days later, these men in dark suits and sunglasses show up on my doorstep askin' to talk to Billy. It seems several people were healed that night and they though my Billy had something to do with it."

"And?"

"And, I told 'em no. He was only a kid – a normal teenager really – but he loved God and people seemed to light up around him. I don't know. He was different than most teenagers, but he definitely couldn't heal anyone." She paused and twisted the hand towel into a nervous knot and gave a bewildered laugh. "I mean if he could heal, doncha think he woulda healed his own brother, first?"

Kristi could see the next word on her lips. "But?"

The woman heaved a sigh and closed her eyes. "But, then they offered me a hundred thousand dollars to let them take him to their lab. I told him he couldn't heal nobody and that it would be a waste of their time. But," she drew the word out, "they insisted."

"And you had another child who could use the medical care that money could buy."

Kristi's soft words brought tears to Mrs. Dunn's eyes. "Yeah, and I've felt guilty ever since. Like I was trading one son for the other." She looked up, grief etched plainly on her fragile features. "You've got to believe me, though. I had no idea he would die. I just thought that they would take some blood, run a few tests and realize he was just normal kid. The next thing I know, they're telling me his heart stopped and he's dead." Her voice caught on a sob.

Tears flowed freely now and Kristi's heart ached for the woman. "And you didn't go to the police or anyone?" she questioned softly.

Mrs. Dunn shook her head and heaved a sigh. Her hand quivered as she used the small towel to wipe her face. "No, I didn't. They didn't ask for their money back and I didn't offer it. I guess I figured they owed me. Then one day about a month after Billy died, this handsome young man shows up on my doorstep. He was all worried about me going to the cops or whatnot and asked what it would take to keep my silence on the reason Billy was at MiracleCorp. Now, I'm not a big thinker, but I was that day. I told him MiracleCorp had to take care of my other boy, Dwayne, for the rest of his illness. He agreed real quick like and has been sending me a monthly check for five thousand dollars."

She gave a weak shrug. "Maybe that makes me an awful person, but it was the only way I could get good care for Dwayne. Billy was dead and there wasn't anything I could do for him. I just hope God can forgive me one day."

"It doesn't make you an awful person, Mrs. Dunn." The three adults turned to see Grace standing in the doorway. "And God would forgive you if you asked Him to. All you gotta do is ask Him. He says, "no" sometimes about some things, but never about that."

Mrs. Dunn's throat convulsed. "I wish I could believe that, honey, but I done some pretty rotten things in my life."

"That's okay, Jesus knows all about that, but he'll still forgive you if you ask Him. That's why He died on the cross for us."

Kristi didn't know what to think about this little girl. One minute she was grossed out at the thought of having to eat liver and onions and the next she was spouting the plan of salvation. David looked a little stunned himself.

"How did you learn all that?"

"Well, my Granma is always talking about Him and says how He just wants to love us and for us to love Him. My mommy used to tell me that too, but she died and is in heaven with Jesus now. But the night she died, I asked Jesus for the gift the preacher man was talking about and I asked Him to come live in my heart. So He did and He gave me a gift so I could help other people like he helped me."

Kristi wasn't having any trouble following the conversation, but poor Mrs. Dunn looked a little shell-shocked. Just as Kristi thought that she might should jump in and help Grace out, the woman knelt down beside Grace and started speaking. "You know, my grandmother used to tell me about Jesus when I was a little girl."

"She did? Did you ever ask Jesus to come in your heart? 'Cause it doesn't hurt if you want to. Then you'll never be alone again. Like when my mommy died. I was afraid that I'd be all alone, but I wasn't 'cause I had Jesus. I mean I had daddy and granma, but they were both so busy and sad all the time, so Jesus helped me not be so sad or alone."

From the mouths of babes.

Kristi felt the tears dripping off her chin and didn't bother to wipe them off. David's shoulders shook and Kristi suspected he was having a hard time holding back tears of his own. Oh, what an incredibly special child God had given this man.

"Yes, I accepted Jesus as a young girl, but I guess I lost him somewhere along the way."

Grace reached out and touched the woman's face. "But He's very easy to find again – if you want to."

Mrs. Dunn gave a soft sob and Kristi worked to stifle another one of her own. The woman grasped Grace's small hand. "Oh, I do, honey, I surely do."

Grace gave her a beautiful smile. "Then all you gotta do is ask."

And so she did. Kristi reached out to grasp the woman's hand and watched as she poured her hurts and aches out to the wonderful heavenly father who welcomed His lost child home.

"Daddy, can I pray for Dwayne?"

David was obviously beyond words. He could only offer a shaky nod. Grace gave another brilliant smile and pulled a befuddled, but peaceful, Mrs. Dunn into Dwayne's bedroom.

# # #

Kristi and David followed slowly, anxious, but excited about what they were going to see.

When they entered the bedroom, David inhaled the smell of illness, medicine and several other scents he didn't even want to attempt to identify.

A boy about the age of twelve lay stretched out on the bed with an oxygen tube running from his nose to the canister on the floor. He was frail and pale, but his listless eyes brightened when he saw Grace re-enter the room. Apparently she had made a friend.

"Dwayne, this is Mr. Walton and Ms. Henderson."

"Hi," Dwayne's whisper floated across the room. David knew this boy's days were numbered. His heart pinched with pity for this family. Looking at the boy, he could understand this mother choosing money over justice. He didn't agree that it was right, but he wasn't sure he wouldn't have done the same thing in her situation.

Grace walked over and picked up Dwayne's hand. "I'm gonna pray that Jesus makes you all better."

"Do you think he'll do it?" The poor child's raspy voice made David's throat hurt just listening to him force the words out.

Grace shrugged. "I don't know. I know He can, so I just ask Him. He decides if He wants to do it or not."

Dwayne's every breath shuddered from his diseased lungs and he shut eyes. Grace seemed to take that as permission to proceed. Her little voice filled the room. "Dear Jesus, this is my friend Dwayne. He's real sick and is gonna die soon if you don't make him better. I know you love him and wouldn't mind him coming to heaven, but I think his mommy kind of needs him here a while longer. Would you please make the sickness go away and make him all better? Thank you, Jesus. I love you. Amen."

Mrs. Harper's excited scream rang out. Kristi had a big grin on her face and Dwayne was looking around with a stunned look on his face. Grace was jumping up and down, clapping and giggling all at the same time.

David blinked, then blinked again. It had been an instantaneous change. A perfectly healthy young boy now sat up in his bed. Grace climbed up on the bed to pull the oxygen tube from his nose and give him a big hug.

Dwayne still looked a little shell-shocked, but was starting to smile. He hugged Grace back with arms now filled out with normal twelve-year-old strength and muscle. All signs of illness and disease had disappeared. His sudden, rich laughter filled the room.

Kristi's face was once again wet with tears. Joy filled her features and David found himself on his knees watching the mother and son with excited abandon.

"Thank you, God, thank you, God, thank you, God." It was a chant he didn't even know he was saying until he felt Kristi's hands embrace his head.

Still on his knees, he buried his face in her stomach and clung to her. He couldn't sort out all of the emotions rushing through him. He needed time and space. But he was sure of one thing. He would never be the same after today. David found himself wanting to know the God who had just answered his little girl's prayer and healed a boy on the edge of death.

David gave Kristi one last squeeze and pulled himself to his feet. He pulled the hem of his shirt out of his pants and used it as a rag to wipe his face and eyes.

"If you blow your nose on that, I'll be totally grossed out."

Kristi's light comment could have seemed out of place, but David knew why she said it. They all needed a breather from the overwhelming power that they had just witnessed. It was almost too much to take in.

David gave a small laugh and let go of his shirt.

"I...I don't know what to say." Mrs. Dunn's tear thickened voice caught his attention. There was a mixture of joy, fear, wonder and just plain bewilderment on her features. "I really don't know what to say." She threw her hands out, obviously frustrated with her loss for words.

David reached out and pulled her into hug. "You don't have to say anything. Just thank God and love your son for the rest of your life."

A look of determination stamped her features. "Whatever you need, whatever it takes, you tell me and I'll offer any help you need. Anything, you hear me? And don't you dare let them people get their hands on that little girl. She's a gift. God has given her to you. I never saw such a thing in my life, but I can tell you this. I ain't never going to be the same again."

Her words echoed David's thoughts. David had never felt so humbled as he did at that very moment. God had allowed him - doubtful, skeptical David Walton - to witness, through his own daughter, a love and power beyond his comprehension.

No, he would never be the same again.

#

Kristi knew without a doubt she would never view life the same way ever again. Sure, she had heard Mike, the bed and breakfast owner, tell her that his little girl had miraculously recovered from the chicken pox. And she believed him. But hearing about and witnessing it were two very different things.

The next morning, they walked out of the Dunn's house after having accepted a teary invitation to stay the night. Mrs. Dunn had just gotten home from a successful errand at the bank and Kristi clutched the documents that proved Billy Dunn had been invited to take part in a special testing session at MiracleCorp labs.

Bank deposit slips in the amount of five thousand dollars each for the past four months were tucked away in the manila folder. The bank had generously provided Mrs. Dunn with copies of the checks and Mrs. Dunn had, in turn, handed them over to David and Kristi.

Kristi knew without a doubt that God was in control. She may not always understand His ways, but she knew she'd never again doubt his love. In this imperfect and sinful world, God was good and loving and only wanted a personal relationship with each one of his children – and he'd do anything to get it; including giving opportunity after opportunity for his wayward children to find their way home to His loving arms.

Kristi felt exhausted and energized all at the same time. She put her seat belt on out of habit; vaguely aware of David and Grace calling their good-byes to the mother and son. David and Grace climbed into the vehicle and Kristi looked out the window.

Dwayne stood, healthy and energetic, on the front porch waving for all he was worth. "Bye Grace! Come back to see me when you can!"

"Bye Dwayne!" Grace called back, giggling at the same time. Her curls bounced along with her little body. She had energy to spare. Kristi wondered how in the world the little girl would endure another long day of driving.

When her cell phone rang, she couldn't figure out what the intrusive noise was at first. She was on such a plane of exuberance, that coming down to answer the phone didn't seem possible. However, on the third ring, she managed to grab the device and answer with some semblance of calm.

"Hello?"

"Hi Kristi. Tess, here."

"Tess, hi. How are you?"

"Good, how about you?"

Kristi smirked and gave a little laugh. "I don't think I have the words to describe it."

"Uh, okay. You can explain that later. I've got to go before someone comes in. I've got another family for you. There was a man, thirty nine years old, who came to MiracleCorp happy and healthy, and left in a body bag."

Kristi landed on earth with a shattering thud. There was still work to do. "Right, okay. Give me the name and address."

She wrote the information down on her palm with a pen she dug out of the storage area between the seats. "Okay, thanks Tess. Oh, before you go, could you do me a huge favor and call my parents? If I don't check in soon, they're going to have the FBI out looking for me. Although now that I think about it, that might not be such a bad idea."

"Ha, sure, I'll be glad to do that. Good luck and I'll be praying for you."

When she hung up, Kristi turned to David. "Are you ready to retrace our steps?"

"Sure, what have you got?"

"A couple who live in Memphis, Tennessee – the Whites. Tess found their names in a similar way that she found the Dunns. Again, there was no information, no paper or computer trail, just a name and a date. Tess was suspicious and suggested we try them. The husband died from a heart attack the very day he arrived at the lab."

"Good grief. It sounds like these poor people didn't have a chance. What kind of testing are they using anyway?"

"Beats me. Tess couldn't find any trace of any tests that were done. From what I can put together, it looks like they find these people at healing services or newspaper articles. Make them an offer they can't refuse to get them to show up – include paperwork and all that to make it seem legitimate and then once they're there, they kill them. Now what kind of sense does that make?"

David shook his head. "Absolutely none. I confess I'm just as confused as you are."

"My brain is starting to hurt."

"So, think about something else."

"Like what?"

"Tell me about your fiancé."

Kristi couldn't speak for a moment. He had done it again. "You did it again."

He grinned at her, then sobered. "Do you mind talking about him? If it's still a painful subject, then don't think you have to tell me about him."

Kristi looked out the window. "No. It's not painful anymore. I think I just have regrets for what might have been. I miss him, but it's been four years. Time really does heal if you let it. And God."

"Yeah, I'm coming to see that." He reached over and took her hand. She was really starting to like it when he did that.

"God's working on you, huh?"

"Yeah, I guess He is. You haven't done a bad job yourself."

Kristi raised her brow and shot him a look. "Oh?"

"You know, we've known each other all of what – five days? And I feel like I've known you for much longer than that."

Kristi laughed. "Well, you can't say those five days haven't been packed full of excitement and drama."

David snorted. "That's one way of putting it." His expression gentled and he stared at her for a minute. "You've changed my life."

Her heart thudded and she swallowed hard. "I'd think this experience would be enough to change anyone's life."

"True, but having you to share it all with," he paused and looked away for a brief moment, "well, I don't want to think what would have happened if you hadn't been there."

"David, I...," she started to tell him exactly what would have happened if she hadn't been there. He, Grace and his mother would be safe at home getting ready for the Christmas holidays.

"Christmas!" Kristi blurted.

"Excuse me?" David looked totally confused.

"Christmas," Kristi insisted, "is only two weeks away." Oh Lord, please tell me we'll be home for Christmas.

Now David looked shocked. "Well, so it is. And you're not getting out of answering my question that easily."

It was her turn to be confused. "Pardon?"

"You were going to tell me about your fiancé."

"I was?"

"Kristi." The exasperated look on his face pulled her pity strings and she gave a small chuckle. "Okay. Michael was a great guy. He loved life, loved people, loved me." Memories rushed in and she smiled. She missed him, but the sharp, aching wound had healed. "He was a police officer. Killed in the line of duty by a strung out junkie."

"Sheesh. I'm so sorry."

"Yeah, me too. I visit his grave once a year. On the day we were supposed to be married, June the fourth. We met in Med School in Charleston. How we ever found the time to date, I'll never know, but we did and we fell in love. He worked the streets by day and took classes at night. He was just getting ready to quit and go to school full time when he was shot."

David's hand squeezed hers and she squeezed back, grateful for the contact. "Sounds like he was a great guy."

"Yeah, he even became a Christian about three months

before he was killed. That's what makes his death bearable now. Knowing that he's in heaven."

David was quiet for a moment; his voice was sad when he did speak. "For some reason that didn't give me much comfort when Lydia died. I was too mad at God for getting to be with her when Grace and I were left with nothing. Didn't seem fair."

"Life's not fair, that's true. But God does promise that no matter what happens, He'll never leave us nor forsake us. His grace is infinite and abundant."

"Yeah, I know that, but sometimes, that just doesn't seem like enough. I guess I'm learning that I don't have the right to know all the answers. That God does things in his own time and reveals himself in his own way. Maybe I just have to accept things the way they are and move on. Maybe that's why he's put you in my life. To teach me that."

Kristi smiled around the guilt eating at her. "I don't know why we had to meet like we did. I'm sure God has his reasons."

In fact, she wouldn't mind knowing them herself.

Chapter 10

"This is all my fault, isn't it?"

James whipped his chair around to see Pamela standing in the door to his office. Tears streaked mascara down her cheeks and smudged under her eyes. She had aged five years over the last month.

"What do you mean?" He knew what she meant, but he couldn't face the possibility that it was her fault because then he was afraid he might hate her. But he couldn't hate her because he was as responsible for her choice as she was. After all it was his money that had allowed her to follow through with the decision she had made all those years ago.

Pamela closed the door softly; James barely heard the click. She glided over to the sofa on the opposite wall and sank gracefully onto it. Her slight frame barely made a dent in the cushion. She'd lost too much weight over the last several months. Tinted blond hair was piled into an artistic mess on top of her head. James never did understand how she kept it from tumbling down. One of those female things, he supposed.

She leaned back and sighed. Her eyes wouldn't meet his; instead she stared at a spot on the ceiling. "Oh, James, you know what I mean. Is God taking our son away because of what we did? What I did?"

"I don't want to talk about this, Pamela." He shuffled papers that didn't need shuffling.

"Well I need to talk about this. I need some answers." Her voice was unnaturally sharp and James stared at her in surprise. "I can't bury myself in work and forget the world going on around me. I don't have that luxury." Bitterness oozed from her and he felt his jaw drop. He hadn't realized that's what she thought he was doing.

"Pamela, I ...," he didn't know what to say.

She held up a hand. "Forget it. I'm sorry. You have to deal with this your way. I just want to know if God is punishing us for...before."

She couldn't even say it. And James truly didn't know. He'd asked himself the same question so many times in the last few years, he had lost track – and he still didn't know the answer. He sighed. "I don't know, Pamela. I truly don't. I've been studying the bible, though."

"I know. I've seen you when you don't know I'm watching. Has it helped? Have you been enlightened in any way? Has Seth gotten up and walked? Has he been healed? No."

He couldn't help but catch the sarcasm, but didn't have the energy to respond to it. Besides, he knew she had to get some of the anger out of her system before it poisoned her totally. So, he rolled with the punch.

"Obviously not. But I can't help wondering if what Jesus is talking about is more of the fact that although we have troubled times, we can get through them if we rely on Him to get us through them. I haven't come across anything that says anything about Him promising a great life to those who follow Him. But one verse did stick out in my mind. It was in the book of Joshua. He said, 'I will not fail you, nor forsake you.'"

"James, get your head out of the clouds. The only way we're going to have a miracle, the only way our son is going to live is if you find that child and get her here."

"I'm working on it. In fact, I'm taking great care that I stay on top of all that Geoff's doing. He keeps saying he's found someone, then they don't work out. They end up dead."

Pamela looked truly shocked. "You can't mean to say that you think Geoff had anything to do with that?"

James looked her straight in the eye. "Yes, I can say that I think he would do something like that. There's something dark about Geoff. Always has been."

"You're paranoid," Pamela snapped. "You need to forget about him and concentrate on finding that girl to save our son!" The tears started flowing again, and the only thing James knew to do was to walk around and hold her. She clung to him desperately – and he let his own tears mingle with hers.

The jarring of the phone broke them apart. James cleared his throat and scrubbed a hand across his face. He needed a shave. Pamela gave a sad little wave and walked out the door.

James snatched up the phone. "James Sinclair."

"Hello Mr. Sinclair. This is Debbie Herschel in personnel."

"Yes, Ms. Herschel, what can I do for you?"

"We have an employee that's been missing for several days – not reporting to work or bothering to call in - and her boss thought you should know about it. He's writing her notice now, but we know how you want to personally be aware any time there's talk of firing an employee – publicity and all that."

"Yes, yes, you did the right thing. Who is she?"

"Um…Kristi Henderson."

James bolted upright. "Kristi Henderson?"

"Yes, sir."

"Thanks and don't do anything just yet," James ordered. "I want to track her down and talk with her myself."

"Oh, okay, sir. I'll wait until I hear back from you. I'll

also let her boss know what's going on."

"You do that. Thanks." James dropped the phone back in the cradle.

Well, well, Kristi Henderson. Missing the same time as the father and daughter. There had to be a connection somewhere. She had been working the case – and now she had disappeared.

He grabbed the phone and punched in a number he knew by heart. When the voice on the other end answered, James stated, "Carl, I have a job for you to do and do right. My brother has screwed it up and I'm running out of time. I want you to trace all numbers – home, cell, work – and credit card transactions for the name Kristi Henderson. Right. And I want it yesterday."

# # #

The drive back to Memphis was uneventful. David decided to take his time, as they all needed a break from the riding. They stopped often and tried to make the day as enjoyable as possible for Grace. Her laughter was his reward.

The only kink in his day was the fact that he felt compelled to constantly look behind him. Was someone following them? Had they found them?

David finally convinced himself he was being paranoid, but cut himself some slack about it considering the circumstances. He enjoyed watching Grace and Kristi bond and delight in each other's company.

Grace had missed her mother and it showed in the way she blossomed beneath the umbrella of Kristi's undivided attention.

"She's getting attached to you, you know." He placed a hand on her back as they walked down the steps to see the monkeys.

Kristi smiled up at him and a wistful smile floated across her lips. "I know. It's quite mutual. She's a truly delightful child." Grace mimicked the monkey scratching his head and hooting. Davie and Kristi laughed at the duo's antics. Kristi's smile lingered and she told him, "You've done a wonderful job with her."

The compliment felt good. "Thanks. Mom's tried to take Lydia's place – or at least make up for her absence, but she's older and doesn't have the energy some days to keep up with her."

"Grace'll be fine, David. You'll see. God has a plan somewhere in all of this."

"Hm. I guess we'll see, won't we?"

"Have faith, David, have faith." Her voice was a gentle command and David was once again in awe of her unflagging trust.

"I'm working on it, Kristi."

She laughed. "Actually, I think it's God who's working on it."

David didn't disagree.

"Daddy, come look! Tigers!" Grace raced ahead; David and Kristi followed at a more sedate pace. He never let her out of his sight, though. David wished he could pretend that this was just a regular family outing, but couldn't take the chance, so he watched over Grace and over his shoulder.

"Daddy, Kristi," Grace bounded over to grab them both by the hand and pull, "let's get some ice cream. I want chocolate and raspberry swirl."

David raised an eyebrow in Kristi's direction. "What's your favorite?"

Kristi grinned at Grace. "Chocolate and raspberry swirl."

The look on Grace's face was stunned surprise at first, then she burst into sweet little girl giggles. "You're teasing me."

"Yeah, I am." Kristi reached down to tickle Grace, who

squealed and took off toward the ice cream stand twenty feet away. Kristi followed right after her.

David grinned at the two of them and shook his head. What he wouldn't give for a lifetime of hearing the two of them laugh.

When they finally reached Memphis, it was getting dark, so they decided to wait until morning to make their visit to the Whites. David bid Kristi goodnight and slid a sleepy Grace between the sheets of one of the two double beds in the hotel room.

He sank onto the other bed and pulled off his shoes. Another hotel room. They all smelled the same. It was an odor he couldn't explain other than he was glad he could smell the cleaning solution used. He wondered if he'd ever get the scent out of his nose. He was ready to go home; sleep in his own bed. Work in his workshop in the backyard.

Take Kristi out on a date.

Find someone to love her as much as I do.

Was it possible? Could he have fallen in love in the span of a week? Or was he just drawn to Kristi because of their unusual circumstances? And could he possibly trust God with his whole heart once again? Would God even forgive him?

David sighed. Yes, God would forgive him. If he had learned anything at all over the last couple of days, it was that God would forgive him – all he had to do was ask. But did he even want to do that? Why was he so uncertain? Trust. It was a trust issue.

And he knew where to go to find the answers.

David slipped out of the room to knock on Kristi's door. He hoped she wasn't asleep yet.

"David, hi. Is everything all right? Is Grace okay?" She stood in the doorway blinking owlishly at him, obviously surprised to see him.

"Uh, yeah. Everything's fine; she's asleep. I just came to

ask if I could borrow something." Why was he having such a hard time asking? He shuffled his feet.

She smiled at him and his heart did a little two-step. David cleared his throat, then blurted, "Could I borrow your bible?"

She didn't hesitate. "Of course." She left the door standing open while she retreated to pick the open book up off the bed. She had been reading it.

"If you're not done with it, I can come back later." David wasn't real sure that this was what he wanted to do anyway. He could still back out of reading it.

But Kristi was having none of that. The pleased look on her face told him he would be going back to his room with the book. She plopped it into his hands. "Please, help yourself. I've been praying for you, David."

Somehow that didn't surprise him. Her next words however, did. "Why don't you read Proverbs chapter three?"

He looked at her. She was so beautiful, her features softened by the light behind her. Her hair a wondrous mass of tumbling, silky curls. He wanted to bury his face in them. She had managed to climb into his heart and he realized that he was dreading the time he would have to say goodbye to her.

His hand seemed to have a mind of its own as it reached out to gently cup her cheek. That cheek turned a rosy shade of pink and David thought it incredible that a woman could still blush in this day and time.

"Kristi, I...better go." He had to get out of her before he said or did something he'd regret. Disappointment flashed briefly in her eyes before she covered it up with a smile. When she stepped back, David felt a sense of loss that he couldn't explain. He only knew he had to have some answers first.

"Okay, David. I'll see you in the morning."

He smiled at her. "Sure. Proverbs three, right?"

"Right."

"Right."

She smiled again, recognizing he was stalling. "Night, David." She shut the door in his face.

David shook his head and headed back to his room. He had some reading to catch up on. Not to mention the possibility of mending a few fences with his heavenly father.

Back in the room, he set the bible on the nightstand, then checked on Grace. She was sound asleep, worn out from the day's activities. He brushed his teeth, then looked at the phone. Should he call his mother?

You're stalling, Walton.

Giving in to the inevitable, he stacked the two pillows against the headboard, then sat on the bed and got comfortable. Reaching over to pick up the bible, he held it in his hands and stared at it for a moment.

Now what?

Read Proverbs three.

Kristi's prompt had him flipping through to the middle of the book. His previous years and training in church hadn't left him as far as knowing where the book of Proverbs was located.

David found the third chapter and started with verse one. And felt like God smacked him between the eyes.

"My son, do not forget my teaching, but let your heart keep my commandments; for length of days and years of life, and peace they will add to you."

David sucked in a deep breath. Is that why I haven't had any peace? Because I've forgotten your teaching? Because I've turned my back on you?

He continued reading with verse three. "Do not let kindness and truth leave you; bind them around your neck, write them on the tablet of your heart. So that you will find favor and good repute in the sight of God and man."

When David came to verses five and six, a lump

formed in his throat and tears began to edge their way to the corners of his eyes. "Trust in the Lord with all your heart and do not lean on your own understanding. In all your ways acknowledge Him and he shall make your paths straight."

I need to learn to trust you again, don't I? To let you heal me. So much emotion flowed through him, peace flooded him and he knew that God was listening. And then verses eleven and twelve brought him to his spiritual knees.

"My son, do not reject the discipline of the Lord, Or loathe His reproof, For whom the Lord loves, he reproves, Even as a father, the son in whom he delights."

Reproof. God wanted his attention; for David to sit up and take notice; to repent of his anger and rebellion; to come home to a father's loving arms.

Oh God! I'm so sorry. Please forgive me and help me work through the anger, and the bitterness.

David grabbed a pillow to smother his sobs. As the pillow soaked up David's tears, his heavenly father held him and soaked up his repentance. Crying had never felt so good – and he didn't feel one bit of shame for doing so. God did love him. God cared and God hurt for him. David's soul drank in God's presence like a starving man and he relished the comfort that was offered.

David offered up one last prayer before he drifted off. And thank you for placing Kristi in my life at just the right time.

# # #

Wednesday morning dawned early and clear. Kristi woke with the sun streaming in through the crack in her curtains. She never could get hotel curtains fully closed. It had made her feel vulnerable, but she had been too exhausted to worry about it. She had slept deep.

They would visit the White's today and see what else they could gather against MiracleCorp.

MiracleCorp. How had she been so wrong about James Sinclair? When Kristi had continued to see his name in the tabloids and the good deeds his company contributed to, she had been proud to work there. Of course she had other reasons for jumping on MiracleCorp's job offer two years ago, but the company's spotless reputation had just been the icing on the cake.

Only now, that icing was sliding off like hot lava, exposing the core of the company and it's evil under layer.

Kristi derailed that train of thought and decided to have her quiet time and get her shower before David came knocking. Then she remembered that David had her bible. The absence of the book unbalanced her for a moment.

Then the idea that David might possibly have gained some answers to some of his questions the night before sent a rush of satisfaction through her. Well, she could shower and pray at the same time.

Thirty minutes later she was packed and ready to go. It was going to be a long drive. Kristi felt sure once this adventure was over and done with – assuming she lived to see the end of it – she'd be quite willing to stay close to home. She mentally canceled any future road trips. Yep, staying home was quite fine with her.

Before she could stop it, the mental picture of the three of them, David, Grace and herself, sitting in front of her fireplace and sipping hot chocolate, danced enticingly across the edge of her mind. Kristi shivered at the idea of the three of them possibly becoming a family.

Then reality came crashing down.

David would never be able to handle her part in putting his family in danger. He hadn't caught her blunder yesterday, but if he thought about their conversation, he would be sure to remember what she had said about visiting her fiancé's grave once a year.

June fourth.

Only the day she had run into David and Grace had been a chilly day in October – barely two month's ago.

Would he put it together? Had her subconscious been feeding him a clue, hoping he would ask her about it so she would be forced to tell the truth?

The sudden knock startled her out of her internal analyzing. She hurried to the window to check on who it was. It was probably David, but right now, she wasn't taking any chances.

Grace. The little girl stood patiently waiting for Kristi to open the door. Kristi obliged.

"Hi there. You and your dad ready for another day of riding?" Kristi forced her voice to sound cheerful; like riding in a car for the next eight hours was something she was looking forward to.

Grace rolled her eyes. "I don't know if I'm ready, but I guess that's what we have to do, huh?"

Kristi smiled and decided to be honest. "Yeah, I know what you mean. Actually the thought of getting back in that car makes me want to…uh…," her voice trailed off.

"Barf?" Grace supplied helpfully.

Kristi laughed out loud. "Yeah, that's a good word for it, although I don't know if your dad wants you to use it."

"Well, you have to agree it doesn't sound very ladylike." David's deep voice interrupted their girl talk. When her heart thumped with a mixture of joy and sorrow, Kristi realized that she loved to hear the sound of his voice. Somehow she had to back off or she was going to be wounded beyond repair once David discovered her deception.

"Sorry, Daddy." The impish light in Grace's eyes canceled out the verbal apology.

David reached out and ruffled the little girl's golden curls. He offered a reluctant smile. "Although, I guess it is a pretty accurate description of how we all feel about more time the car, huh?"

That brought Grace's impishness into full-fledged laughter. The laughter lingered until they were all buckled into the Suburban.

"Here." David handed her the bible he had borrowed the night before. "Which way?" David asked.

"Toward Memphis. Once there, I'll read the directions to you. You need to get on I-40, though."

"Okay, here we go."

"Yeah, here we go." Kristi echoed. She caught David's glance out of the corner of her eye, but decided to ignore it. "So, did you read Proverbs three?"

"Yup."

Kristi saw a small smile slide across his full lips. He was either being deliberately obtuse or was trying to tell her gently that he didn't want to talk about it, yet. Whichever was fine with her just as long as he had read it. Two could play that game.

"Oh. Good." She leaned her head back and closed her eyes. The silence stretched into several minutes before David's hearty laughter had her eyes shooting wide open. "What in the world is so funny?"

"You are!"

"Me? What'd I do?"

"You would sit there all the way to Memphis and not ask me what I thought about the passage, wouldn't you?"

"Oh," Kristi smiled, then let out a small chuckle, "yeah, I probably would."

"Why?"

The amazement in his voice surprised her and she gave a small shrug. "I guess because I figure you don't want to talk about it right now, but when – and if - you're ready, you'll share it. I mean, times with God can be mighty powerful and personal. I'm not going to push you into sharing that. It's not my business."

David shook his head. "You're amazing. I've never met anyone like you before. It used to drive Lydia nuts when I wouldn't tell her something."

Kristi noticed that for the first time, the pain that used to shadow his eyes when he spoke about his wife wasn't there. What was she supposed to say to that? She settled for, "Hm."

"God really spoke to me last night." His voice was soft, all hints of teasing gone. His eyes reflected an inner peace. No, they weren't out of trouble yet, but David had come a long way last night.

"I'll listen if you want to share."

His smile sent shivers all over her. Oh, God, I'm falling for him. I've got to tell him everything. But how, when? Help, please.

Kristi listened as David shared the intense experience he and God had had the night before. "I'm back on track, Kristi. I don't know all the answers. I don't know why everything that's happened in the last few weeks has happened. Maybe it was God's way of getting my attention. I wish I hadn't been so stubborn, then maybe He wouldn't have had to work so hard, but his persistence has won me back. I can't imagine how I've made it this far without Him."

"That's because you were never without Him." Kristi couldn't help interjecting that point. True, David had pushed God away, yet at the same time he had been begging God not to give up on him. And God had listened. He had given David his space to make his mistakes, but had been close enough to pick him up when David finally asked for his help. How like a loving father.

"Yeah, I guess you're right."

"Of course I am."

"Ah, the good doctor. You always do things right and never make a mistake, huh?"

Kristi winced. "Oh, I make mistakes all right. And sometimes I'm at a complete loss as to how to make them right."

# # #

David wondered what she meant by that comment, but after she had dropped that bombshell on him, she'd leaned her head against the window and shut her eyes – effectively shutting him out.

The eight hours finally passed with only two stops for food and bathroom breaks. When the welcome to Memphis billboard finally whizzed by, David wanted to stop the car and have a good stretch.

Kristi had entertained Grace and him for several hours by making up funny stories about different animals, then Grace had fallen asleep an hour ago, tired of hearing stories, reading and doing word searches.

David couldn't believe how good she was being. So far, she hadn't really whined or fussed about the long hours in the car, but he could tell it was taking its toll on her. It was taking its toll on all of them. Something had to break soon. He just hoped it wasn't his heart. David glanced over at Kristi, who had fallen asleep about the same time Grace had.

Her beauty never failed to make him shake his head in wonder. She was falling in love with him, he could tell. And she cared enough about him to encourage him to get his heart right with God before openly encouraging him to act on his own feelings. The thought that he could love again without guilt brought a lump to his throat. He cleared it loudly.

"Huh? What?"

His throat clearing had startled her. "Sorry. We're here. Can you tell me which way to go?"

Kristi gave a yawn and rubbed her eyes. "Sure. Where

are we?"

"Uh, I was hoping you could tell me."

"Oh. Okay." Kristi fumbled in her bag for the directions she had written down earlier. "Keep going on I-40, then get off on the next exit and make a right."

Kristi continued to give him the directions until they were stopped outside a brick house in a middle class neighborhood. David took in the well-manicured lawn. In the spring it would be a magnificent yard; the brown of winter not hiding the obvious loving care this home had been given.

"Daddy, can I come too?"

David turned to see Grace peering up him, her blue gaze still a little foggy from her nap, but determined not to be left out. He smiled.

"Sure, honey, we're all going." He walked around to the passenger side and opened Kristi's door. He held a hand out to help her out of the car and thought how right her hand fit in his. He enjoyed the brief contact and silently craved more. "Ready?"

"As I'll ever be." Her words were distracted; her mind obviously already inside the house with the widow.

David led the way up the walk to the front door. Three smart raps brought the sound of light footsteps the paused just inside the door.

"Who is it?" The voice was husky, cultured, and a tad curious.

"David Walton, Mrs. White."

The door opened silently and David found himself staring down into friendly green eyes. "Yes? May I help you?"

David cleared his throat and wondered how to begin. Thankfully, Kristi took the decision out of his hands. She stepped forward and extended her right hand. "Hello, Mrs. White. I'm Kristi Henderson and this is David Walton and his daughter Grace."

Those green eyes widened slightly and her mouth

formed a silent, "Oh."

Kristi let out a small laugh, "Yes, oh, is one way of putting it. I take it you know who we are?"

"Yes, I've seen you all on the news." Her eyes lowered to Grace. "Hello, sweetheart. Aren't you an angel?" Grace grinned up at her. The woman paused then stepped back, opening the door a little wider. "You don't look like dangerous criminals. Please, come in."

"I can assure you that you are in no danger from us." David hastened to tell the woman. She merely smiled and led the way through the house to the sunroom located in the back. Mrs. White gestured to two comfortable looking wicker chairs and matching sofa. David took the sofa and Grace scrambled up beside him.

"Can I get you anything to drink? Eat?" She hovered in the doorway, ready to turn back into the kitchen.

"Oh, no, please. We're fine."

Mrs. White clasped her hands together and pulled them against her chest as she sat in the chair opposite David and Grace. "Well, then, what can I do for you?"

David looked at Kristi, silently asking her to begin. She nodded. "Mrs. White, I'm not really sure where to start or how to say it, so I'll just be blunt with you if that's okay."

"It's more than okay; it's preferred. Now, what's on your mind?" She was obviously a woman who didn't ruffle easily. Kristi plunged ahead.

"We are on the run from a company named MiracleCorp..." Kristi repeated the story they had shared with Mrs. Dunn. "Would you mind sharing how your husband ended up at MiracleCorp?"

"No, I don't mind. But first, Grace, there are some books in that trunk over there that belong to my grandchildren. You're welcome to plop in that big ole bean bag and read while we grownups chat. Would you like that?"

"Sure," Grace responded eagerly, probably anxious to

get away from all the serious stuff she knew that was to come. With Grace settled, Mrs. White turned back to Kristi and David and began.

"My husband was a dear, gentle man. He had a deep, abiding faith in the Lord and really believed that God would heal. That he still healed today, just like he did so many years ago when he walked the earth. Often, parishioners would come to him and request prayer for healing."

"But he never actually healed anyone?" David questioned.

"No, of course not. Not he, himself. Now, God often answers prayers and a lot of the people that my husband prayed for got well, but not in a way that would consider as a miracle healing."

"Well, what do you mean? If they got well, then God healed through your husband's prayers, right?"

"Yes, but I mean, he prayed for them if they were sick and gradually they would get better. These people also went to the doctor and got medicine and did what normal, sick people do. I'm sure the prayers helped, but they were by no means miraculous healings. People pray all the time for others to get better, to heal, and they do."

"But MiracleCorp obviously felt like there was something more to those prayers and approached you and your husband, right?" David scooted forward to the edge of his seat.

"Yes. My husband gave an interview for the religion section of the local newspaper. He talked about faith and prayers and how God still miraculously heals even today. The two men who came to see us had a copy of that article in hand."

David and Kristi exchanged glances. David still wanted to know more. "How did they approach you about coming to the lab?"

"At first, they were very pleasant. But my husband continued to declare that he did not have the spiritual gift of healing. He insisted that God didn't use him to miraculously heal people, although Christopher believed that God could heal should he choose to do so. Then they turned a bit nasty."

"Did they offer you any money?"

"Oh, yes, quite a bit, but we refused it."

"Then what happened?"

Mrs. White's throat convulsed. "They threatened our grandchildren."

David jumped to his feet and slammed a fist into an open palm. "Those dirty, rotten…"

"Sit down, young man." Her voice was soft, but the words were a command. David sat.

The woman leaned her head back and closed her eyes. "Christopher decided that he would go along with them; prove to them that he had no power to heal, and simply come home. He never made it home. He had a heart attack the day he arrived. I suppose the stress was just too much for him."

David grunted. "Something was too much, that's for sure. Did they leave you any papers of any kind?"

Mrs. White looked startled for a minute, then stood to walk over to a desk in the corner of the sunroom. "You know, they did. When Christopher refused the money, they handed him the papers and told him when he changed his mind, to sign them and bring them with him. Christopher stuck them in this drawer and I've not thought about them since. He never took them with him, obviously."

After thanking the woman for her help the trio ended up walking out of the house with a set of papers equivalent to the ones already in their possession.

"Mission accomplished." David grinned, relief and weariness vying for first place.

"Yes, now don't you think it's time to call in the reinforcements? We can't keep running like this and we need to stop these people before anyone else winds up dead."

"You think they'll believe us?"

Kristi handed the papers to him. "All we can do is present them with the evidence and leave the rest up to God."

"Sounds like a plan to me."

Chapter 11

Unfortunately, even the best-laid plans can get derailed.
When Kristi finally got ahold of Tess, she was stunned
to hear Tess tell her that she was wanted by the FBI.

"I'm what?" She knew her screech probably had Tess
holding the phone away from her ear, but she couldn't help it.

"You're wanted for kidnapping by the FBI. It was on
CNN last night. Fox news carried it too."

"But how in the heck did they come up with that one?
How did they connect me with the Waltons at all? And did
they say anything about David?"

"Nope, not a word about David and Grace. And I don't
know how they knew you were with them. Somebody has
put it all together and come up with the right answer, unfortunately. Hey Kristi, hold on, will you?" Kristi heard Tess in
the background asking someone to turn down the television.

"Tess? Who's there with you?"

"It's the new man in my life." Kristi heard the love
struck sigh in Tess' answer.

"Ah, well I don't want to keep you. I'll let you get back
to your love life. Great, now what am I going to do?"

"I don't know, hon, but you can't keep running forever.
Maybe if you call them, they'll cut you some slack and listen to what you have to say."

Kristi let out a sigh and glanced over at David. He was

stretched out on the bed with Grace beside him. They had decided to stop at hotel for the night because they could hardly stand the thought of getting back into the car for the trip home.

One more night. One more day. And hopefully this nightmare would be over. Kristi felt the evidence that they had was rather flimsy, but she really didn't know what else to do.

She had the papers to prove a link between the deaths of two people that MiracleCorp had contacted and brought onto their property. Kristi hated it, but unfortunately, it looked as though James Sinclair was guilty of murder. Hopefully the evidence she had would be enough to open an investigation. If not, well, she hated to think about it.

Plus, she really needed to come clean with David and let him know how all of this got started in the first place.

"All right, Tess. Thanks for the information."

"No problem. So, what are you going to do now?"

"We'll spend the night here in Memphis, then head on back to South Carolina in the morning. I am so ready for all of this to be done with."

"How's Grace holding up?"

Kristi felt the love for the little girl well up. "She's a trooper. And Tess, she really can heal."

"For real?"

"For real. I saw it with my own eyes."

"You're talking about that little blind kid, aren't you?"

Kristi was startled. "How did you know?"

"Kristi, turn the news on. I can't believe nobody has spotted you and turned you in yet."

"God must be pulling out all the stops on protecting us."

"Just keep praying and I'll do the same. Stay safe. You might want to think about finding another vehicle. They've got yours broadcast all over the news."

"Well, that's just great. Okay. I'll call you later."

"You know you need to ditch that phone. It's beyond me that someone hasn't traced that number yet."

"It's prepaid, nothing to trace."

"Ah, good thinking. All right, take care."

"Thanks Tess, and make sure you keep yourself out of trouble."

"You too, bye."

Kristi left father and daughter sleeping and walked back to her room. Unfortunately, there were no connecting rooms available, so she had to go outside in the cold and walk two doors down.

She scrubbed her clothing in the sink while her thoughts drifted to how to tell David the truth. She could picture the scene.

"David, I have something to tell you. It's all my fault someone is trying to kill you and your daughter."

Oh yeah, that would go over well.

Or, how about, "David, the reason people know about Grace is because I found her and led them straight to you."

Nope. Please God give me the right words and the right timing. And please put forgiveness in David's heart.

# # #

"They're at a motel in Memphis, Tennessee."

James clutched the receiver in a death grip as though that would help him get his hands on the one person he was convinced that could provide his miracle. "How do you know? Are you sure?"

"That's what you hired us for, sir. We're sure."

"Can you get to her?"

"They're headed back this way, so our best bet is to check the motels along I-40. They're also still driving her car – a black SUV. We've traced all her credit cards and so far have come up with nothing except a large cash withdrawal a couple of days ago. They stopped at a bank and she used her credit card to get a cash advance."

"So that's how they're paying for their impromptu cross country flight?" Frustration ran rampant. Why was it so hard to catch this family?

"I don't know, I guess, unless they've got a stolen card or something."

A harsh laugh barked from his throat. "Kristi Henderson never stole a thing her life. There's no way she'd steal a credit card."

"Whatever you say sir. But desperate times can bring out the survival instinct in anyone."

James sighed. "Truer words were never spoken. All right, get the chopper. Use the satellite tracking system and pinpoint every motel in Memphis, then narrow the search down by choosing ones along I-40. Once you've done that, you can trim the search to anyone who checked in requesting two rooms. Every hotel we've tracked them to so far has shown that they get two rooms. From there, you can scout the motels in the helicopter, checking out each one that contains a black SUV."

"We need a pilot. Should we call Geoff?"

"No, I'm not sure I trust him anymore. Get the tracking done and I'll have a pilot at the helipad in thirty minutes."

"Yes sir, we're on it."

"And don't screw this up. I don't want a hair on that child's head hurt. Do you understand?"

"Absolutely sir. What about the father and the girl-friend?"

James hesitated only slightly. "I would prefer that they not be harmed, but do whatever it takes to get the little girl here – and try not to scare her to death in the process. Remember, she's just a little girl and I desperately need her help."

"Got it. We'll report back to you as soon we've got her."

James hung up the phone and leaned back in his chair. A glance at the clock on his desk showed him it was only seven thirty. He had an overwhelming urge to visit his son.

Excitement warred with worry. Would they be able to get her here in time? The doctor's were saying Seth could go at anytime. He still registered brain activity, but he was now on a respirator; the click and whoosh of the breathing apparatus the only sound in the room most of the time.

Occasionally the nurse would play some of that Christian music that talked about heaven and angels and a loving, awesome God.

More and more, James found himself listening to the words and praying to a God he wasn't sure existed. But hoped did. He had been reading in Hebrews eleven. "Faith is the substance of things hoped for, the evidence of things not seen."

James entered the bedroom and nodded at the nurse, his unspoken question causing her to shrug and say, "There's been no change, sir, good or bad."

"Why don't you take a break while I spend some time with Seth."

"Sure, I'll just be down the hall. Let me know if you need anything more."

James nodded gratefully. He had come to appreciate the woman he had been so bitter about. But she treated Seth like a son, her movements gentle as she cared for him, filled with sincere concern.

James ignored the smell of sickness and antiseptic, as he looked down at the wasted body of his son. Anger, fear, bitterness, and... a small grain of hope tumbled around inside him. It was like his mind and heart couldn't focus on one emotion.

"He's hanging in there."

James didn't bother to turn at the sound of Geoff's voice; he just continued to stare down at Seth. "Not for much longer though."

"I can't find her James."

"I know." James picked up the twisted, limp hand of the boy and ran his fingers over it. He remembered when that hand had been so tiny and perfect.

"Come on, Daddy," three-year old Seth had begged as he grinned and pulled on James' hand, "come push me on the swing!" How Seth had laughed and giggled as James had pushed him as high as he dared without giving Pamela a heart attack.

James thought about this same hand that had loved to cast a line out into the water. Even at five years old, Seth had been a skilled fisherman; knowing all the names of the different species and what lures would attract what kind of fish. It hadn't seemed possible that he had some disease that would one day kill him.

Pamela had first noticed that Seth walked on his tiptoes shortly after his second birthday. At his three year old check up, the doctor grimly announced that their son had Muscular Dystrophy and would probably only live a few years.

His muscles would eventually stop working and he would need a wheelchair to get around. Then would come the point where he would struggle to breathe and would eventually stop breathing all together. All they could do would be to make him as comfortable as possible in his last days.

James didn't realize he was crying until the teardrops landed on Seth's hand. Grief was the dominant emotion now.

"So, I guess there's nothing more we can do, right?"

James clenched his jaw at Geoff's words. A good punch in Geoff's nose would make him feel so much better. But he restrained himself and sucked in a deep breath, hoping to conceal what he was feeling.

"I'll never give up, Geoff. Not until Seth is gone. As long as there is brain activity, I'll never give up. This is my

son. My flesh and blood and I'll never stop fighting for
him." James stared into his younger brother's eyes and the
sorrow there made him flinch. Then the sorrow changed to
a look James had never seen before; a look he wasn't sure he
could put a name to. Geoff's next words were quiet and
calm, but held a scathing contempt that all but took his
breath away.

"It's a shame I was never given the chance to fight for
my flesh and blood, isn't it, brother?"

James wilted and had nothing more to say as Geoff shut
the door behind him. The fact that he didn't slam it hurt
more than if Geoff had stood there and beat him with a baseball bat.

# # #

Kristi pulled on her jeans and a sweatshirt the next
morning. She had placed them near the heater after rinsing
them out the night before so everything was dry except for
her jeans. They were still slightly damp, but nothing she
couldn't live with.

Rain drizzled outside giving the day a gloomy feeling,
but inside, her heart beat with excitement and dread.
Excitement that this ordeal was almost over and dread
because she knew it was time to tell David the truth.

Last night she had fallen asleep to the sound of her bedside radio tuned to the local Christian station. She had
ignored the helicopter passing by overhead.

After her morning quiet time, she could no longer put it
off. When she read the words in John about the Holy Spirit
- "He will guide you into all truth…" - she knew it was time.
God was a God of truth. She would have to trust Him in all
things – including telling David everything.

"All right, Lord. I need you to give me the words, guide
me in what to say and how to say it. I'll tell him in the car

on the way to the police station."

Five minutes later she was rolling the clothes she had washed out the night before into a plastic bag provided by the motel, when she heard a light knocking.

After the initial jolt of fear, she realized that it must be Grace and smiled as she headed to answer the door. The eagerness she felt at seeing the little girl brought home to her heart just how much she had come to love this father and precious daughter.

The thought of once again being in David's company all day was exhilarating, even if the conversation she needed to have with him scared her to death.

As her hand touched the doorknob, the scream from the other side had her heart thumping in fear and her blood racing in terror. "Grace!" She threw open the door to see Grace being dragged through the rain and shoved into a gray sedan with tinted windows.

"Kristi! Daddy!"

Grace's screams spurred Kristi on toward the car. Adrenaline pumped her feet faster and she managed to grab the handle of the back door. She punched the window with her other fist, but it was no use.

The vehicle sped away slamming Kristi to the asphalt. Gravel and dirt chewed the tender skin of her cheek, and her shoulder bounced painfully against the ground. Ignoring the stinging injuries, she jumped up and ran for David's room.

"David! David! Where are you?" Kristi realized she was sobbing hysterically as she pounded on his door. "Come out now! They've got Grace!"

The door flew open and David stood dressed only in a pair of jeans. His hair dripped water on the floor. He had obviously been in the shower during all of the commotion. Sheer panic looked out at her from his blue eyes as he grabbed her arm. "What do you mean they have Grace? What happened to your face?"

"They just grabbed her! Hurry, get dressed, we've got to catch them." She wiped the tears and blood from her cheeks as she paced and waited for David to finish dressing. He handed her a wet washcloth to help. Thirty seconds later, they were in her car heading west on I-40. Wipers chased each other back and forth across the windshield making the road visible for David.

"Go to the airport." Kristi barely held the terror at bay as she watched the needle pass the one hundred mile per hour point. Her terror wasn't that he was driving too fast, but terror that he wasn't going fast enough. "Oh, please God, keep her safe. Let us find her. Don't let her be scared. Comfort her." Kristi didn't realize she had been praying out loud until she felt David's hand clutch hers in a brief squeeze. He quickly returned it to the steering wheel.

"Why am I going to the airport?"

"I don't know. I don't know." She pressed the cloth against her cheek again. When she pulled it away, it was saturated with her blood. She probably needed a couple of stitches. Kristi pressed it back and held it, hoping the pressure would help stop the bleeding.

"I just feel like that's what we're supposed to do. It's the only way they can get her back to South Carolina with any speed – and if MiracleCorp is behind this which we know they are - speed will matter. They'll know we're coming after her and they know we won't have access to flights. Not with our faces plastered all over the news."

"Right. Okay, the airport it is."

They whizzed back and forth in the traffic drawing angry honks from other motorists. Kristi finally told him he was going to have to slow down. They couldn't afford to be stopped and possibly put in jail. Grace needed them to find her. David complied seeing the wisdom in her words. The drive seemed to take forever when in actuality it only took about twenty minutes.

"David, stop." They were on airport property when Kristi looked up into the sky and noticed a helicopter flying fairly low. It held the MiracleCorp logo. "Look."

David pounded the steering wheel and tears dripped down his cheeks. His hands shook and Kristi felt her heart rip in two at the anguish reflected on his face. "Oh God, please keep my baby safe. Now what do we do?"

The whispered words held a wealth of emotion and Kristi couldn't bear to look at his pain anymore – not when all of this could have been avoided if she'd just followed her conscience in the first place. If she'd only listened when she felt God was telling her that James Sinclair was not the man she thought him to be.

She said, "Go straight to James Sinclair's house. I'll show you how to get there when we reach South Carolina."

"How do you know where the CEO of MiracleCorp and kidnapper of my daughter lives?"

Kristi swallowed hard. "It's a really, really long story."

"You can tell me on the way."

#

"They're on the way, Pamela. They're on the way." James could hardly contain his excitement. When he smiled, his muscles protested. It had been an eternity since he'd used them last.

Pamela simply looked at him, doubt and despair too thick to let any other emotion in, much less anything close to excitement or euphoria. "You mean Geoff found her?"

James barked a harsh laugh, all merriment fading from his face. "Not hardly."

"What do you mean?" Pamela frowned, confused. "I thought you had Geoff looking for her?"

"I did, but we both saw what a disaster that turned out to be. No, I have my own guys working on this now. This is too critical. Until I'm sure I can trust Geoff, I'm going to have to do this by myself." James walked around the desk to stare out the window. The gray clouds exuded a somber mood and a light rain fell gently to the ground. Normally, such a day would have been a reflection of his mood, however, with Grace's imminent arrival, not even the dismal weather could halt his rising excitement. "They should be here anytime."

"You really believe this girl can heal Seth, don't you?"

James swung around to face the woman he loved so much. It made his heart break to see how Seth's illness had changed her. Gone was the laughter, the simple joy she took in the small things. In their place had grown bitterness and anger. How he longed to see her smile again, to hear her laughter ring out in the house. Sure, she had made some mistakes in the past. They all had. But everyone had gotten past them; moved on. Hadn't they?

"I believe she can. I have to believe it, Pamela."

"How did you find her?"

James sighed, but answered honestly. "I got a call from personnel. They were getting ready to fire an employee due to unauthorized leave. Apparently this person just took off and didn't tell anyone where she was going. She also didn't bother to call into work and let anyone know she would be gone. This particular person was working on the case, tracking this little girl and gathering information. She disappeared the same time they did."

"Who is it?"

James ignored the question and continued his story. "I had the guys do a little checking and they found out she has a best friend in the department she works in. I forget her name, but I had them tap her phone and last night we hit pay dirt. Although they didn't talk long enough to trace the call completely, we got a pretty good estimate of the area where they were staying. Some more hi-tech searching and I sent in the helicopter. We picked her up this morning. The little girl came out of the room and the boys snatched her." He shook his head and muttered, "Shoulda done that in the first place."

"James! That's kidnapping!" Pamela looked stunned, completely aghast at what he had done. James felt shame flare briefly, but the thought of his deathly ill son upstairs quickly squelched the emotion. "We're not going to hurt her, just see if she can do what's been reported. If she can't, she's free to go on her way. But if she can," he paused and his throat worked before he could get the rest of his sentence out, "if she can, then we get our son back."

"Oh, James. I can't believe you've stooped this low. Kidnapping!" Pamela got up to pace and James grabbed her arm.

"She could heal out son!" The shout echoed through the office. Pamela shrank from his verbal assault and yanked out of his grasp.

Bitterness poured freely from her lips. "And you could ruin us all! Then where will I be? Seth dead and you in jail? What will I do then?"

James couldn't stop the words that escaped. "I suppose you would always have Geoff to fall back on."

All fight was gone from her. Her face drained of any color that had been there and a small wounded whimper escaped. The tears cascaded down her gaunt cheeks and she whirled away from him to throw herself face down on the couch.

James immediately castigated himself and had to work to stop his own tears from falling. Why couldn't he control his tongue? He had no desire to hurt this woman, and yet at times she made him so mad he spoke before he thought.

James dropped down beside her on the couch and his fingers made their way into her hair, pulling the strands out of the loose bun. Pamela allowed him to offer the small measure of comfort but still her tears fell. He pulled her into his arms, desperate to take back the words he never should have let pass his lips.

"I'm sorry, Pammie. I'm sorry. I just don't know how much more I can take." James reverted back to the nickname he hadn't used since Seth had become ill.

Slender shoulders continued to shake and James just held on to her, hoping she would forgive him once she stopped weeping. Slowly, she gained control and pulled away from him. Sorrowful, wet eyes peered up into his. "You'll never forget will you? Or forgive? I don't love him, James. I never did. I just did something incredibly stupid – and I've paid for it, several times over, I believe. Haven't I suffered enough? Do you and God both think that I need even more punishment? Is that why this is happening?"

"No Pamela, no. I can't believe that. I won't believe that. Nothing in the Bible leads me to believe that God is a hateful, punishing God. Apparently, He disciplines us. And while He does forgive, He doesn't necessarily take away the consequences of our actions. So, no. I don't believe you need more punishment and I can't believe the God I've been reading about believes that either."

Confusion and sarcasm dripped from Pamela as she spat, "But you believe He will condone kidnapping?"

James swallowed and looked away. No, he didn't believe that God would condone his actions. In fact, James was pretty sure that he would have some serious consequences to face before all this was over, but if there was even the slightest chance that this little girl could heal Seth…

"What's going on? Is Seth all right?"

Geoff's appearance jerked husband and wife to face the door as one. Pamela began repairs to her appearance and James got up to face his brother. "Nothing is going on. And Seth is the same. Still dying. It's just hard, you know?"

Geoff laughed, but the sound lacked humor. "Yeah, I know."

"What are you doing here?" James asked. Pamela motioned that she was going to go back upstairs to be with Seth while the two men talked and James nodded his acknowledgement. She slipped out the door, silent as a wraith.

Geoff walked over to James' desk and picked up a pen. The look on his face was an odd one, one that James couldn't put a name to. He questioned Geoff again. "What are you doing here? I thought you would be in the lab."

Geoff set the pen down. "I was. I couldn't concentrate. I was thinking about when we were kids. You always came out ahead of me in everything, didn't you?"

James wondered where this was going. "What do you mean? I'm nine years older than you are. I'm supposed to come out ahead of you in some things."

"True. And you always beat me in everything, including love." Geoff's voice was oddly introspective. James had never heard him talk like this before and he didn't like it. Before he could question him, Geoff continued. "I have someone I'd like you to meet. She's coming for dinner tonight. Of course once she meets you, she may decide to dump me. I guess this will be the real test of true love, won't it?" Geoff laugh, but there was no humor in the sound.

Time to change the subject. "Geoff, I need you to get a..." The sound of an approaching helicopter chopped off the rest of his sentence. James felt his blood rush to his head and for a moment he felt dizzy with euphoria. Seth's miracle was landing on his roof.

"What's that?" Geoff's frown was directed toward the ceiling.

"That, my dear brother, is a little girl by the name of Grace Walton who apparently has the spiritual gift of healing and is here to heal my son."

Shock registered. "She's here?"

"In the flesh."

"But how?"

"Never mind how. It's done and you don't have to worry about it anymore."

Geoff cleared his throat and regained his composure. "Well, that's great James. That's great. Once again you managed to outdo me, huh?"

"You're talking crazy, Geoff. Now who is it you wanted me to meet?"

"My girlfriend. Theresa MacDougall. But you can call her Tess."

Chapter 12

"Faster, David."

"I'm going as fast as I dare. And besides, you're the one with the good advice. No getting stopped by the cops, remember?" White knuckles glared at Kristi from their position atop the steering wheel.

"I know, I know. I just…" She bit off the words and sank her teeth into her lower lip. Kristi dabbed at her scraped cheek one more time. The bleeding was slowing. Maybe she wouldn't need stitches after all. She flexed her shoulder and winced. Not dislocated, but definitely bruised. Her hip ached with a dull steady throb. Sitting hurt, standing probably wouldn't feel so great either. Tomorrow was going to be a nasty day for aching and bruised muscles.

David spoke taking her mind from her pains. "They're going to be there several hours ahead of us. No telling what they'll do to her before we get there." His voice broke and tears slipped from his already tear swollen eyes. Kristi knew he had just about reached the breaking point. He slammed a fist on the steering wheel and ground out between clenched teeth, "Why is God doing this to her? Why doesn't He just take that gift back and leave her alone?"

"I don't know, David. I don't even pretend to come close to understanding the mind of God. But surely, He has a plan in all of this. Don't stop believing now."

"No way. I have to believe. I just don't understand." David whipped his way around another car, then shot back into the right lane.

Kristi shut her eyes, then opened them and said, "Give me the cell phone. I'm going to call Tess and ask her to go over to the Sinclair mansion and see what she can find out. See if she can find Grace."

David passed her the phone and Kristi punched in the numbers while her mind raced. Could Tess go over there and find the little girl without exposing herself to danger? Would they hurt Tess if she arrived on the doorstep? Would they even let her in the house? Should she try talking to Pamela or James? No, that wouldn't work. That might make things worse.

"Hello, this is Tess."

"Tess, Kristi here. We need your help."

"What? Are you okay?"

"They've got Grace." Kristi almost choked on the words.

"Oh, Kristi, no. How?"

"I don't know how, and can't really worry about that right now. Right now, we need you to get over to the Sinclair mansion."

"What? Why?"

"Because I think that's where Grace is going to be taken once they land. We saw the MiracleCorp helicopter take off from the airport. I know the mansion has a landing pad on the roof. As much as I hate to admit it, if MiracleCorp is behind this, you can bet James and Geoff Sinclair are right there with them."

Silence greeted her from the other end. "Tess? You there?"

"I can't believe...I'm here. Just thinking."

"About what? Are you willing to help?"

"I'm thinking about the Sinclairs. Are you sure that Geoff has something to do with this?" There was some kind of plea in Tess' voice that Kristi didn't have the energy or time to try and label at the moment.

"Ninety nine percent. Why?"

"Because you remember that new man in my life?"

Kristi wondered why Tess was bringing up her love life right now, but managed an affirmative answer while keeping her eyes peeled for the highway patrol.

"Well, his name is Geoff Sinclair."

Kristi was sure her heart came to a complete halt before picking back up with an erratic rhythm. "Come again?"

Tess didn't bother to repeat herself. They both knew Kristi's stunned question didn't need an answer.

"Tess, how could you?" Kristi tried to keep the accusation from her voice, but failed miserably. "No, never mind. I just need to know one thing. Can we trust you to help us? Or are you convinced that Geoff isn't involved in this?"

Tess stumbled over her answer. "I-I-don't know. I just can't believe that he would be involved in something to hurt anyone."

"Just remember that two people involved with MiracleCorp have ended up dead. Now, who do you suppose would be involved in that?"

"I don't know, Kristi. I truly don't know what to think. Geoff is so charming and kind and...I just can't believe that he would do something so...evil." Tess' voice sounded choked, like she was trying to hold back the tears. "I can't believe that I could be such a bad judge of character."

"I don't know what to tell you, Tess. Maybe he's not involved in it, maybe it's just James, or even an unknown person, but I need to know if you'll help us."

A sigh shuddered through the phone into Kristi's ear. "I'll see what I can do."

Kristi pressed the end button and disconnected the call. Would she help them? Or warn the Sinclairs that David and Kristi were on their way? The dashboard clock to her she'd know the answers to her questions in about four hours.

Kristi took a fortifying breath and turned to the man beside her. "David, there's something I need to tell you."

#

She was here. Grace. The little girl that could heal his son. James swallowed hard as Pamela's words still rang in his mind.

Kidnapping.

A shudder ripped through him and he pushed the thought away. No, it wasn't really kidnapping. He wasn't going to hurt the child. Nobody was going to hurt this child. Kidnapping was taking with the intent to get money out of someone or with the intent to hurt someone. He just wanted to borrow her for a bit. That's all. His intent was to help someone. Then he'd give her back. Surely it wasn't really kidnapping - was it?

Of course it was. He couldn't rationalize the wrong and make it right. He had kidnapped a child. James swallowed hard then squared his shoulders. If this child could heal his son, James would gladly spend the rest of his days behind bars.

The helicopter sounds faded as the blades churned to a stop. James stood statue still on the roof, his hand raised to shield his eyes from the glare of the sun. His stance denied his intense desire to rush forward and grab the child as soon as she disembarked.

All of his senses were on hyperalert - the warmth of the sun on his face, the chilly breeze whipping from his left. The fumes from the helicopter burned his lungs with every breath. And finally, the sound of the engine being shut down made him shudder.

Then everything faded as the door to the aircraft opened. James stared into the yawning black hole; his breathing quickened in anticipation of what was to come.

Finally.

Carl, one of the men who had found Grace, appeared in the opening and hopped lithely to the ground. He turned and held up his arms.

James sucked in a deep breath as he watched a small body edged toward the open door. And there she was. Her body language fairly shouted resistance, but she placed her hand in Carl's and let him help her to the tarmac.

Carl propelled her toward him with a gentle hand on her back and when she finally stood before him, James found he couldn't speak past the clog in his throat. Carl spoke first. "Sir?"

James cleared his throat and somehow he found his voice. "Yes. Hello Grace." He held out a hand. She crossed her arms and stared at him, defiance and fear written all over her. James shuffled and dropped his hand.

As he looked into her eyes, he felt - ashamed. He hadn't expected the guilt. Taking another fortifying deep breath, he shoved the guilt aside, reminded himself that he was doing this for Seth, and knelt to meet her eyes. He said again, "Hello."

"Hi." She spoke quietly, warily. "Are you gonna kill me?"

The words punched him in the stomach; guilt returned full force. He forced a reassuring smile and stated, "No way. I'm going to take real good care of you, and then give you back to your Daddy, okay?"

Hope lit her blue eyes, but her expression remained skeptical. "Really?"

"Really. I promise." James needed her cooperation, not her fear.

Her lower lip quivered. "I just want my Daddy." Tears hovered on the edge of her lashes, threatening to spill down her cheeks.

James sighed and forced another smile. "Come on inside

and we'll get you something to eat and drink. Then you can see my son and see if you can heal him. He has a horrible disease and is real sick. Once you do that, I'll give you right back to your Daddy. Deal?" Seth had hung on this long. He could hang on a few more minutes until she was more comfortable.

Grace didn't answer, she just stared up at him. James took her hand without another word and let her to the stairs that would take them down into the main house. He was barely able to hold himself in check. He wanted to take her straight to Seth and demand that she heal him. But first, he had to make her understand that he wasn't going to hurt her.

Grace followed him silently although tears still trickled down her cheeks every once in a while.

"James?" Pamela's voice brought him to a screeching halt.

"Hi Pammie. Guess who I've got here?" He made his voice cheerful for both of the females. "This is Grace. Grace this is my wife, Pamela."

Grace stared up at the woman without moving or speaking. Pamela stared back, her gaze unblinking, then she asked, "Can you heal my son?" The words were blunt, straightforward and filled with too many different emotions for James to identify.

Grace shuffled her feet, then looked his wife straight in the eye. "No."

James thought he was going to throw up. He stooped quickly to her level. "But you have healed. Remember the healing services and the little blind girl. You healed them."

Grace shook her head. "No, not me."

Anger, fear, and sheer terror battled it out inside James' heart. Before he said or did anything rash, he turned to Pamela. Her white, stricken, face stared back at him. Empty. All hope had fled. James could see that even though she hadn't truly believed the little girl could heal Seth, she hadn't been able to stop herself from holding on to one small kernel of hope that maybe she was wrong.

James said no more as he silently escorted Grace to the last room on the hall. The room directly opposite of Seth's. "Stay here for right now. I'll have some food sent up. After you eat and rest a bit, we'll talk some more."

"What's going on? Is that her?"

Geoff's untimely interruption irritated James, but he shook it off and answered curtly, "Yes, and I don't want anyone bothering her right now."

"Well, what did she say? Can she heal Seth?"

James shut the door on Grace's tear streaked face and startling blue eyes. He was glad to get away from them as he felt like she saw into his very soul. When he turned to head back down the stairs to his office, Pamela was standing there, accusation blaring from her taut features.

Instead of lambasting him, she turned without a word and head down the hall to her private sitting area. He almost wished she had ranted and raved. At least then he could have vented his own frustration by telling her to leave him alone.

James turned back to Geoff and ran a hand over his weary eyes. "I don't know. She says no."

Geoff lifted an eyebrow, a funny expression crossing his face. "Really? You mean we went to all this trouble for nothing?" Anger rose as the red in his neck made its way into his cheeks. "What about all the news reports and witnesses that say she can – and has? What about those?"

James shrugged, his heart breaking for his son, his family. "I don't know, Geoff. I just really – don't know." He hung his head for a brief moment, then made his way down to his office - which he had come to think of as his sanctuary.

"Hello? Is anyone home?" The feminine voice stopped him in his tracks. Who in the world?

"Tess?" Geoff's incredulous response answered James' question.

"Geoff? Are you up here? Oh, thank goodness. The woman downstairs told me I could find you in a study somewhere and gave me directions, but I'm completely turned around."

Geoff walked around the corner to lightly embrace the beautiful woman standing before him. James was instantly intrigued, not to mention relieved. He hadn't seen Geoff take an interest in anyone for years. Not since Pamela had broken his heart. The woman standing before him was definitely a beauty with her Hawaiian features and statuesque build.

"What are you doing here? You're early," Geoff said.

"I know. I drove to make sure I could find it, then saw your car sitting in the drive. When I stopped at the gate, the guard saw my name down for dinner tonight and went ahead and let me in. I hope that it's not too presumptuous of me." Her forehead crinkled at the thought and James stepped in to reassure her.

"Absolutely not. It's just fine. Geoff, why don't you take your guest downstairs to the living room. I'll take care of my other guest and we'll visit."

"Other guest?" Tess' innocent gaze collided with James'.

"Ah, yes. The daughter of a friend is staying with us for a short while. I just need to check on her and then I'll be right down. I'll also let Pamela know she needs to come meet you." He shot Geoff a warning glare. Geoff got the message and though he frowned, placed his hand on Tess' back and guided her toward the living room.

James reached out and opened the door that led to Grace's room. She sat on the edge of the bed staring forlornly at the appetizing spread in front of her. The cook had delivered a delicious dinner sure to tempt a six year old appetite. Hamburgers and French fries, a chocolate milk shake and a peanut butter cookie. How could she resist?

She hadn't taken a bite.

"What's the matter, honey? You don't like hamburgers?" James made his voice hearty and happy.

Grace nodded her head and whispered, "Yes, I like hamburgers. I'm just not very hungry right now." Those blue eyes rose to meet his. Tears had dried to silvery white tracks on her pale cheeks. "When do I get to go home to my Daddy? Please, I want to go home." Her lower lip started quiver once again and more tears made their way to the surface.

James steeled his heart against the pitiful sight. "Grace, you can go home just as soon as you heal my son. I know you can do it; I've watched all of the news reports, read all of the newspapers. I know you can do this."

"But it's not me. It's…"

James interrupted. "I don't want to hear anymore denials. The sooner you heal my son, the sooner you can get home to your Daddy, understand?"

Her curls fell forward to cover her face as she dropped her head; a slight nod her only response.

James continued, "Let me know when you're ready by pushing that button on the night stand. When you push that button that means you're ready to heal and I'll come get you and take you to Seth."

Grace didn't bother to respond this time and James left without another word.

She would heal his son - today.

#

Geoff wanted to hit something. Once again, James had bested him. He had found the little girl first and brought her here. He never could win against the man.

"Geoff, what's going on?" Tess asked.

"What do you mean?" Geoff responded, his hand still in the small of Tess' back as he escorted down to the living room - or the parlor as Pamela called it.

"Things seemed a little tense when I walked up. And who's the guest James was talking about?"

Geoff thought fast. "She's no one special, just a kid visiting with James and Pamela. Don't worry about it."

"Well, what's her name?"

Geoff shot her a dark look. "What's with all the questions, Tess?"

Tess shrugged, "No reason, just wondering if the little girl was Grace Walton."

"Yeah, it's her." He didn't see any point in lying. She already knew it was her.

Tess stopped and looked him straight in the eye. Geoff stared back, trying to read the emotions he saw in her eyes. He couldn't figure out what she was thinking. She questioned, "Why is she here, Geoff?"

"Tess, it's really none of your business."

"None of my business? After everything I've done for you? It's none of my business? I won't let you hurt her. I won't let her end up dead like the others."

Geoff just stared at her. "Do you really think that I'd do that?"

Tess looked at the floor, then back at Geoff as she whispered. "I don't know what to think anymore. You said you were trying to help. You just wanted to help. You said she wouldn't be hurt."

"And she's not. She's perfectly fine up in that room right now."

"But what about later? Her father doesn't know where she is. He and Kristi have been running with her for a week now. Call him and tell him where his daughter is and that he needs to come get her."

Geoff stared at Tess. She knew too much. She could ruin the foundation - and him - if she let this get out. "Tess, I promise I won't let anything happen to Grace, okay? I'll make sure James takes good care of her and after he sees that she can't heal Seth, he'll just let her go. Okay?"

"You're sure?"

"She's already said that she couldn't heal him. It's just a matter of time before James sees it for himself." Geoff shrugged, seemingly unconcerned with the whole matter.

Tess' shoulders relaxed. He had her trust again, he could see when she made the decision to believe him. She said, "All right, Geoff. Just be sure that nothing happens to that little girl and that you call her father right away to let him know she's here and fine."

Geoff leaned down to press a cool kiss to her cheek. "All right, Tess," he soothed, "no problem. Come on, let's go down to the study and we can take care of that now."

Chapter 13

David's silence rang loudly in the car. After Kristi's announcement, he had glanced at her, then back at the road. Finally, he spoke. "I've had a feeling you've been hiding something from me all along. Are you sure I need to hear this?"

"Pretty sure."

"Am I going to like it or is it going to add stress to my already stressed out nerves."

Kristi blew out a sigh. "Probably stress you out more."

David nodded. "Yeah, I kinda figured that. Okay, so lay it on me. I've already gone through a whole range of emotions in the span of minutes. Now might be a good time to tell me as I'm feeling kind of numb about everything at the moment."

Kristi drew in a deep, fortifying breath and felt tears prick her eyes. *When I am afraid, I will trust in you. Please Lord, let me be doing the right thing.* "I've known James Sinclair a long time. Actually, it might be more accurate to say that I've known about James Sinclair for a long time. Mostly, by his name appearing in the newspapers, and some from social functions hosted by him for MiracleCorp employees. I've always held the highest respect for the man."

"Until now."

"Yes, until now. When we started this pursuit, I really

had in mind to clear his name. I just didn't think it was possible that he would be involved in something so heinous."

"What?" The word exploded from David's lips.

"Just hear me out, please."

Silence was her encouragement to continue. "But the evidence we have clearly points to him being involved in the two deaths and the kidnapping of Grace. I recognized one of the men in the car. I've seen him around the corporate offices more than once. He and James would also often eat in the restaurant downstairs." She paused and swallowed hard. "And I can't help cover that up, or support that, no matter how much I might want to."

"Why on earth would you want to help the scum who snatched my daughter?"

Kristi winced, "Because he's my brother-in-law."

# # #

The car swerved and Kristi had to grab the dash to keep from being thrown against the door. "He's your what?" David kept his voice calm with a fierce effort. Right now he was seeing red when he really needed to see the road.

His brain finally calmed down enough to focus on her words. "You know that older sister I told you about a few days ago? Well, she's married to James Sinclair."

"And you've just now chosen to tell me this?" Fury nearly choked him.

"Telling you wouldn't have made a difference. I wasn't going to let anything happen to Grace no matter who my family might be, but I was afraid if you knew about the relationship I had with the man trying to get your daughter, you would have run without me."

"Darn right."

"And how far do you think you would have gotten?"

David didn't answer. Couldn't answer. He refused to

acknowledge that she might be right. Not when she'd lied to him all this time.

"Anyway," she went on, "when Pamela was a teenager, sixteen years ago, she got pregnant. My parents were – harsh – to put it nicely. They kicked her out of the house and basically disowned her."

"What? Why? It's not like it's the unforgivable sin."

Kristi let out a humorless laugh at that pronouncement. "Oh, yes it is. At least in my parent's eyes anyway. No daughter of theirs would dare bring shame on the family name."

"And when she did…"

"They didn't know the meaning of unconditional love, or forgiveness. They certainly didn't know Jesus." Kristi took another deep breath and grabbed the door handle for support as David swerved around another car. She went on, "And unfortunately, I didn't either. So I cast judgment on her too. And we've never heard from her since."

"But?"

"Then one day while still in Med School, I desperately needed a break from the grueling pace. You can't imagine the stress, the pressure. I just wanted to get away. So, I took a walk downtown and came across a newspaper stand. I decided to grab a paper and a coke and prop my feet up at an outside café. Finally, I was reading the newspaper and there she was right in front of my face announcing her engagement to James Sinclair, CEO of MiracleCorp. My sister, now Pamela Sinclair."

"Wow."

"Yeah. I decided right then that I would try to get in touch with her. I had long since forgiven her – like it was up to me to forgive anything. I just wanted her to forgive me. And I wanted my big sister back." Kristi raked a hand through her hair, wincing as her fingers snagged tangled curls.

"Did you get in touch with her?"

"Oh yeah. And got the door slammed right in my face for my efforts. Then about six months later, MiracleCorp came calling. I saw it as my chance to get close to my sister. She saw me as a gold digger."

"You?" As angry as he was with her for keeping this information from him, he still couldn't picture as a gold digger.

"Yeah, me. Anyway, I continued to try to get her talk to me, meet with me. She would have none of it. She returned my letters unopened and hung up on me if I called." A tear leaked out and David refused to let himself act on the desire to brush it away.

"So then what?"

"So, then when all this happened I decided that if I could prove that James wasn't behind it and caught the people who were, Pamela might find it in her heart to forgive me."

David hated the anguish reflected on her face, but he was still furious with her, so hardened his heart. "And now you have proof that he is behind it. Are you going to turn it over to the appropriate authorities?"

"Of course." She looked startled – and hurt - that he would even question that.

David gripped the steering wheel. "Kristi, if anything happens to Grace…"

"I know, David, I know and I can't tell you how sorry I am that all of this has happened. Just keep praying."

"I haven't stopped."

They rode on in silence.

#

While David seemed to lose himself in his thoughts, the scenery flashed by unseen for Kristi as she wondered if she dared to finish the story. There was still quite a bit she hadn't told him. Had he had enough or could he stand the rest of it?

Better to wait awhile; give him a chance to mull over and process everything she'd just laid on him.

Racing to the Sinclair home stirred up suppressed memories. When Pamela had been a teenager, she'd been wild. Rebellious. She hated anything that confined her. And their parents had definitely been confining. Then one day Pamela had come home, shaking, sick, and in tears.

She'd announced her news at the family meeting. "I'm pregnant."

Silence reigned like the eye of the storm, then the explosion came. Her father hadn't minced any words as he'd called his eldest daughter every name in the book, ending with Pamela being a prostitute of Satan himself.

"Who's the father?" he'd finally demanded when he'd caught his breath.

"It doesn't matter. I don't love him."

"Get out." His final words were quiet, but the wrath behind them unmistakable.

Pamela wept. "But where will I go, Father?"

"Go to the bed of the father of your child, go live on the streets. Go to hell itself, but don't ever darken this door again because you are no longer my child."

Disbelief filled Kristi as she watched the drama play out. "But...," she'd tried to protest on behalf of her sister..

"And you!" Her father roared to her. "Let this be a lesson to you, girl. Watch and learn, daughter, or you'll find yourself out in the street with your jezabel of a sister."

Kristi sat, stunned. She couldn't fathom that her father would do this. Yet, she could. She knew how he was. She'd felt the slap of his hand on her face often enough. Now she would be alone, her sister gone. She would be the one to bear the brunt of her father's anger and religious tantrums. Her own anger stirred, and she glared at Pamela. "How could you do this to me?"

Pamela glared right back through her tears. "I didn't do

anything to you!"

"You should get out. You knew better. I'll never forgive you for this." After those final words, Kristi had left the room. She'd never discovered who the father of the baby was, nor what had happened to the child.

She must have dozed because David was shaking her back to awareness as they crossed the South Carolina state line. He looked so weary; his shoulders slumped as though in defeat.

"Don't give up, David."

Grim eyes bored into hers. "Never. I'll never give up. That's my child, my flesh and blood. I'll find a way to save her if it kills me."

Kristi shivered. "I suppose God felt the same way about his children."

"Huh?"

"Think about it. God's children were in danger. Granted it was danger brought on by themselves while Grace is totally innocent in this fiasco. But still, God loved them – us – enough to fight for us. To do anything for us. Including die for us."

David didn't seem to have a comment for that observation, but his eyes took on a thoughtful look as he turned his attention back to the road.

Kristi blew out a sigh and studied the ceiling of the car in silence while her mind raced. Would James hurt Grace? What exactly did he want her for? Was there something personal in all of this or was it just the money that he could make with her that had him blinded to anything and everything else? People would pay top dollar to see a child like Grace if there was even the remote possibility that she could heal them.

There were no answers forthcoming, so Kristi closed her eyes and did the only thing she knew to do at the moment. She prayed. God, only You know how all of this will end up.

Please, please, let it have a happy ending. Reunite father and daughter - and me too, if that's your will.

When the mansion came into view a couple of hours later, Kristi's nerves were shot. Praying had helped her stay focused, calm, but at the sight of the house, peace fled. Her stomach tied itself into knots and only sheer effort kept down the food they'd barely stopped for when both realized the need for nourishment. Passing out from lack of food wasn't going to help Grace.

"How are we going to get past security?" Although his question was soft, David's tightly leashed fury bubbled near the surface and Kristi just prayed he didn't let it go – yet.

"I have my badge from work. I don't know if the guard has been warned that I'm now a traitor or not, but we can give it a try." Kristi dug in her purse and pulled out the badge that had been buried there for over two weeks. It seemed like a lifetime since she had clipped it on her neatly starched white lab coat.

"Go for it."

David pulled up to the guardhouse, stopped and pasted a half smile on his lips. A slight touch to the automatic button and the driver's window slid down.

The guard pulled the pen from behind his ear and stepped out of the little house, clipboard poised. "Help you, sir?"

Kristi leaned around David and flashed her badge. "Hi, I work for MiracleCorp and am here to see James Sinclair."

The guard glanced at the badge, then down at the clipboard. "You're name's not listed on here, Dr. Henderson. You got an appointment?"

Kristi flashed a friendly smile; at least she hoped it looked friendly. "No, I sure don't, but James has something here for me to pick up and I don't want to keep him waiting any longer."

"I'll have to call up to the house. Hold on just a minute."

Kristi's heart beat frantically. She flashed David a 'now

what?' look.

"Uh, sir, I don't think that will be necessary. We'll just give Mr. Sinclair a call ourselves and ask him to be sure to put our names on the list."

Kristi jumped in. "Yes, no need to bother him. He wasn't expecting me until later tonight anyway. That must be why my name isn't there." No way did she want to give James the heads up that she and David were here.

"Oh, ya'll invited to the dinner party tonight?"

"Yes, yes indeed. I'll just be sure to call James and let him know of the error so that we won't have this problem tonight. Thanks so much." She motioned to David to back up.

The guard was still speaking. "But I don't mind...if you'll just wait a..."

Kristi smiled, waved and acted like she couldn't hear him.

David's fist hit the steering wheel and Kristi jumped. She moaned, "Guess that was a bad idea, huh?"

David growled. "Now what?"

"We wait until he leaves, takes a break to go to the bathroom, whatever, and sneak in."

"I don't know if I can wait that long. I'm having horrible visions. I just...," Kristi heard the tears in his voice.

"It's only been a few hours. Surely, she's fine. I mean, he doesn't want her dead or he would have just done that at the hotel." Kristi tried to reassure him, but wasn't sure her words were coming out right. Her mind was racing. How could they get in?

David pulled down the street out of sight of the guard to watch the entrance. Neither one of them could think of a better plan. They argued whether to call the cops or not. David was afraid if the police showed up, they'd move Grace and then they'd never find her. Not that he was sure she was there anyway.

Kristi pulled a pair of binoculars out from under her seat.

"Here, see if you can see anything. I'll try and get ahold of Tess and see if she's had any luck."

The house was situated at the top of a large gently sloping hill and although it was set back from the road, it was visible from the street. The circular drive held a Lexus and a Mercedes parked near the front door. The Mercedes belonged to Tess. Relief and hope mingled inside her. "Tess is here. She's inside."

"Call her and see if she answers her cell phone."

Several tall pines were scattered in the front, but not enough to obscure the view of the house. David kept watch while Kristi dialed the number she had memorized. He settled the binoculars on his eyes and Kristi watched him scan the front of the house. He lowered them. "Nothing yet."

"It's ringing."

"Hello?" Tess kept her voice low.

"Tess? Is she there?"

"Oh, hello, Mom. Listen, this isn't a good time right now. Could I call you back in a bit?"

"Tess, just answer yes or no. Is she there?"

"Yes, yes. Of course I will. Okay, Mom. I'll call you later. Bye now."

Kristi pressed the button to disconnect the call.

"Well?" David's voice was tense; expectation hung all over him.

"She's there."

David wilted back into the seat. "She's there. Okay. Now we figure out how to get inside to get her."

Darkness would be falling soon and Kristi desperately wanted inside. Please, Jesus, comfort her, protect her.

# # #

David could barely contain the rage he felt at the men who'd grabbed Grace. He shivered and pulled his coat tighter around him. He'd turned the car off to save gas. He might need a full tank soon. Hang on baby, Daddy's coming. Lord get us in there – and out, please. Tell her not to be scared.

David grabbed the binoculars one more time. The front of the house was mostly large open windows. So far he'd seen several people walk past, but not a blond headed six-year-old.

Show me what to do, Lord. I'm really trying to depend on you. Keep my faith strong – no matter what happens. It was a hard prayer, but David forced himself to pray it. No matter what happens. He couldn't think of any outcome to this other than Grace safe in his arms.

He glanced over to his cohort. Kristi had her head against the window and her eyes at half mast, but David didn't think she was sleeping. Probably praying. Anger still churned like a raging river when he thought of her deception, but he could also understand why she had done what she had done – a little anyway. It would take some time to get over. Assuming Grace was all right. If not…

"Hey, look."

David looked in the direction she pointed. The guard was shutting the door to the little house and had pulled a key out to lock it.

"He's leaving," David breathed.

"Finally."

"But how are we going to get in? He's locking the door."

"Do you think there's an alarm on that guardhouse?"

Kristi shrugged. "Beats me. Why?"

"Because if not, then I can break the glass on the door. By the time the guard comes back and notices it, we'll be inside."

"Good thinking."

"Yeah, I'm surprised I'm thinking at all. Come on."

As soon as the guard had climbed into his golf cart and headed up the drive, David turned the key and the engine roared to life. He pulled up next to the guardhouse and left it running.

A quick circle around the perimeter didn't reveal any sign of an alarm. A large stone from the rock garden that surrounded the building did the trick and within seconds, glass littered the floor and David had the door open.

So where was the switch to open the gate?

David ran his hands around the little desk, then under it.

Bingo. He pressed the button and the gate began to swing open. Soon he and Kristi were pulling through.

"This is breaking and entering, you know."

"Yeah, so what's he going to do, call the cops?"

"True."

"Besides, you're family, right?" David knew the sarcasm was uncalled for, but the words were out before he could stop them and he didn't feel like apologizing for them just yet. Kristi's hurt silence rang like a gong in his ears. He sighed. It would take time. "Let's just find Grace, okay?"

"Sure." Her voice was a whisper and David felt the pang of regret before he managed to squelch it. He pulled in behind the Lexus and climbed out. Kristi joined him and together they walked up to the massive oak front door. Would it be unlocked?

"Should I ring the bell?" Kristi twisted the ring on the pinkie of her left hand; nervous energy radiated from her every pore.

"No, they didn't have the courtesy to ask my permission if Grace could visit. I certainly don't feel it necessary to ring their doorbell and politely ask if I can have my daughter back." His cold voice reflected the anger he held against the people on the other side of that door.

David reached out and pressed down on the handle. It swung open easily. He glanced at Kristi, "Why bother to lock the door when you're inside a gated community, huh?"

David stepped inside and felt Kristi follow him. "Hello?

Anyone here?"

A woman stepped into the foyer and raised an eyebrow. "Yes? May I help you?"

"We're here to see James Sinclair and see him now. Could you tell him he has visitors?"

"Who should I tell him is here?" A frown appeared, making her forehead crease into deep lines.

Kristi stepped from behind David. "Just tell him that his sister-in-law would like to speak with him."

The woman's jaw dropped. "Who? Sister-in-law? But he doesn't have a sister-in-law."

"Yes, he does. I'm Pamela's sister."

David wondered if this approach was wise, but kept his mouth shut to see what was going to happen. Besides, he didn't have a better idea at the moment.

The woman bustled off to find James and Kristi looked up at David. He couldn't meet her eyes yet.

"Hello Kristi."

# # #

Kristi whirled at the sound of the woman's cool voice. "Pamela." She felt tears well up in her eyes. "Oh, it's so good to see you."

Pamela's iceberg manner didn't melt in the least at Kristi's statement, nor did she seem the slightest bit moved by the tears Kristi knew were visible in her eyes. She bit her lip. How could she reach her sister?

"I've missed you, Pam."

Something flickered in the green eyes that mirrored her own, then died. "I thought I got the message across that I wanted nothing to do with you."

Pain shot through Kristi's heart, but she forced herself not to show it. "Yes, you made that more than clear."

"Then why are you here and who is this?" She motioned

a lazy hand in David's direction.

"I'm here to find a little girl named Grace. This is her father." At the mention of Grace's name and who the man beside her was, Pamela's eyes shot wide open; all semblance of nonchalance gone.

"She's your daughter?" Pamela directed the question towards David who immediately jumped on it.

"Yes, and I want her back now. Just bring her to me unharmed, with a promise to leave us alone, and I won't press charges."

Kristi could tell it was taking every ounce of willpower David possessed not to grab her sister and shake her senseless. The white-knuckled fists were her first clue. The muscle jumping in his jaw was her second. She placed a calming hand on his arm. "Where is she, Pamela?"

"Kristi? Is that you?" Tess entered the foyer. "I thought I heard your voice."

"Pamela, who is this?" James walked up beside his wife then got a good look at his visitors. His face quickly lost all color and he swayed slightly.

"Hello James."

"Kristi." Her name was a one word statement. "Have you called the police yet?"

David answered for her. "Not yet, but I'm real close. All I want is my daughter back. Where is she?" He took a step forward as though itching to get his hands around the man's throat.

James answered coolly. "You have no right to come into my home like this."

Kristi and David both burst into semi hysterical laughter.

Then David exploded. "You want to talk about rights? What right do you have to chase us halfway across the country and back trying to take my child away and forcing us to live the way we have for the last week? What right do you have to use your money and power to track us down and steal my child? What right? What right?" David was screaming now, his face blood red as he shouted down at James.

James swallowed hard and backed up a little. Pamela looked as though she might pass out at any moment and Tess stared bugged eyed at the confrontation.

"Get out of my house." The words were shaky, but calm. James tugged the hem of his jacket; the only sign that he was ruffled.

David narrowed his eyes and glared. "Or what? You'll kill us too?"

James reared back, shock written on his features. "What do you mean? Kill you too? I've not killed anyone. No one has killed anyone."

"Daddy?"

The tense group turned as one to see the little girl fly down the stairs towards her father. Before she reached his outstretched arms, James leapt forward to grab her by the back of her sweatshirt. He pulled her kicking and screaming into a tight hold. Kristi wondered why she didn't notice the gun before it appeared in his hand.

"Let me go! I want my Daddy!"

James held her easily with his left hand while he kept the gun trained on the rest of them. David went completely still and Kristi didn't think her heart would ever beat normally again.

"What's going on in here? I answer a phone call and the next thing I know I'm hearing shouting, screaming and all kinds of stuff." Geoff stood in the doorway, a baffled expression on his handsome features. His eyes went wide as he took in the scene and the gun in James's hand. "James? What are you doing with a gun?"

"Making sure my son gets what he needs. Now, I don't want to hurt her, or any of you for that matter, but Grace is coming with me right now to see Seth." He began backing up the steps, pulling Grace with him.

"Daddy? Kristi?" The fear in her voice wrung Kristi's heart in two.

"It's okay, baby, I'm coming too." David hastened to reassure her.

Kristi stepped forward. "We all are."

"Just don't try to stop her. You understand? Because if Seth dies, I have nothing to lose. Nothing. And I don't want to hurt her, I just want her to heal him."

James backed them all up into the room on the second floor. The door was cracked so he simply shoved it open with the heel of his foot. The nurse was nowhere to be seen.

"Over there." He motioned them with the gun to one side of the bed. He pulled Grace to the other side. "Now heal him."

Grace shuddered. "But I don't know…"

"Just do it!" James shouted at her. "Do it!"

"James…," Pamela offered a sincere protest, but subsided when he ignored her.

"Heal him," he ordered Grace.

Tears leaked from the little girl's eyes as she looked at the wasted young boy on the bed beside her. Her small hand trembled as she reached out to touch him. Then she bowed her head.

"No!" The animalistic scream shocked them all. Geoff pounced over the bed and tackled his brother. David rushed to pull Grace into his arms and bolt for the door.

"Stop! Everyone just stop!" A gunshot sent plaster and wood from the doorframe flying.

Everyone froze. Geoff now had control of the gun.

"Geoff, what are you doing? She can heal my son!" James held his hands out in confusion as he backed toward the bed. "I just want her to heal Seth." Tears began to trail down his cheeks, but Geoff's face was cold, hard and unforgiving.

Kristi broke in, "Then why were you trying to kill them?"

James looked up, confusion still the dominant expression. "Kill them? Never. I just wanted them to bring her here."

"Then why didn't you just ask?" David screamed the question at the man as he kept a tight grip on Grace. Now that he had her in his arms, there was no way he was letting her go.

"I didn't have the chance. You took off."

"Only because Kristi called to warn us that someone was trying to find us and was planning to kill me and...if not you, then who..." David's voice trailed off and they all turned stunned eyes to the man holding the gun. "You?"

Pamela echoed, "You, Geoff? You killed those people, didn't you?"

Tess let out a horrified gasp. "No Geoff, tell them it's not true. You wouldn't do something like that, would you? It was all James, wasn't it? You tried to stop them. Tell them. You were trying to find Grace to keep her safe because you knew he would hurt her just like the others. That's why I let you tap my phone and told you everything I knew. Tell them!"

"Tess?" Kristi was shocked. Betrayed.

"I'm so sorry Kristi, but..."

An evil laugh cut her off. "You're all a bunch of idiots. Kristi is the one who found Grace in the first place. She set you up, Walton."

Kristi couldn't describe the fear that shot through her entire body. He couldn't find out this way. Oh, Lord, please.

"Kristi?" The confusion in his eyes nearly took her breath away.

"It didn't exactly happen that way. Yes, I found Grace and told them about her, but I..."

"That's right, and tell them how you arranged that little meeting in the graveyard and how it was your idea to find out where the little lady went to the doctor so you could set yourself up to have contact with her. Go on, tell them." Geoff sneered. The fact that he was enjoying ripping her heart out made her angry; the betrayed shock on David's face had her weeping.

"You were supposed to marry your fiancé in June," he whispered, "but it was October when we met. But you said you only visited his grave once a year – each June." Realization dawned and his face turned to granite.

Kristi wilted inside, her heart dying a slow agonizing death as the extent of her deception became clear to him. "Yes, but…"

"What other lies have you told, Kristi?"

"None. That's everything I haven't told you. I never wanted to lie to you, but I was afraid…"

"Enough," Geoff cut in.

"Why, Geoff?" This time it was James questioning his brother. "Why?"

"Revenge. Plain and simple. Revenge. Do you really think that I would allow you find someone that could heal your son when you stole mine from me?"

Long suppressed rage bubbled at the surface like an infected wound. James' question seemed to lance it and the infection spewed from Geoff in uncontrolled fury. "You killed my son – my child!"

Kristi and David watched the scene go in another direction. Geoff still blocked the door, so the only option they had was to stand and watch Geoff empty years of hatred onto his brother's head.

"You killed my son, my child," he repeated.

"Stop." Pamela's plea fell on deaf ears.

Kristi thought the woman was going to fall over at any moment. She swayed like a willow tree in a soft wind. Dark circles ringed her eyes and she seemed to have aged ten years in the last two minutes. Kristi grabbed her arm and held her up. Pamela leaned into her; her strength gone.

Geoff continued his tirade. "You and the woman I loved killed my child." He swung to face Pamela. "You used me, then tossed me aside and went running back to him. I begged you," his voice broke and he had to pause to gain control, "and still you went to him. And you," the gun waved in James direction, "you let her. You took her back even after all that she had done to you. She was pregnant with another man's baby and you took her back and paid for her abortion."

Pamela whimpered and Kristi thought she would be sick. Her poor, poor sister. So much suffering. So much needless suffering.

"There is no way I would ever let anyone who had even a remote possibility of healing near this place or your son. He deserves to die! You don't deserve to have him live. So, yes, I killed them. I killed them all. Except for her. But I can remedy that situation now." The gun swung in Grace's direction and Kristi screamed.

When the gunshot sounded, Kristi thought for sure Grace was dead. Grief almost made her black out before she realized that David still stood with his back to Geoff; Grace shielded by his body. James lay on top of Geoff who lay on the floor, blood seeping from the wound to his chest. "I'm sorry, Geoff, but I couldn't let you kill her."

James was now back in control of the gun.

It all happened so fast, Kristi's brain could hardly take it in.

James slowly pulled himself to his feet and looked down at his brother, regret and sadness shining from his wet eyes. Then he turned to Grace.

"Now heal him, child. Do it." His words commanded, but his voice was flat. Hope had no place in his heart anymore.

Grace looked up from her father's shoulder. "Let me down, Daddy."

"No." His arms squeezed tighter.

"It's okay, Daddy. I think I need to do this. Let me down."

David hesitated, then lowered her to the floor. She walked back to her original position at Seth's bedside. The respirator the only sound in the room until Grace's soft voice interceded on behalf of the boy.

"Dear Jesus, Seth really needs your help. If you want him to get better now, could you please heal him?"

All eyes were on the still figure on the bed. Nothing changed. Grace looked up at her father. "I guess God answered my last prayer already."

"What's that baby?" David asked.

Before she could answer, Kristi lifted stunned eyes to see men in uniforms surge into the room. "Freeze, police!"

The nurse stood in the doorway nibbling on a nail.

Over the next several minutes, as chaos reigned, the story slowly came out that she had been in the bathroom next door and had heard the commotion. Thinking swiftly, she snuck down to the kitchen and called 911.

Upon their arrival, officers had stood outside the door and listened to the entire thing. They were waiting for the opportunity to present itself to get Geoff without causing anyone else to get hurt. James just beat them to the punch. Listlessly, he surrendered his gun.

Handcuffs were slapped on Geoff as a precaution; he was moaning about his shoulder. James kissed his wife's white cheek as he passed by her, hands cuffed behind his back, and Kristi heard him whisper, "Don't give up."

One of the agents approached Kristi and she held her hands out expecting to feel cold metal touch her skin. Instead the man reached out to shake her hand. "Guess you're off the hook, ma'am. That confession said it all."

And he left Kristi standing there watching David. He looked up and met her eyes. Without a word, he shifted

Grace to his other hip, turned, and walked out the door and out of her life.

Chapter 14

"**D**addy, are you ever going to forgive Miss Kristi?"
David felt the punch of that question. It had only been two weeks, but he missed her terribly. Christmas had been a dismal family affair. His mother had decided to stay in Italy through the holidays with her sister, so it had just been Grace and him and while Santa Claus had managed to find everything Grace had asked for -not including the horse - the day had seemed rather depressing, neither one in the mood to celebrate much. The day after Christmas, Lydia's parents had driven down from North Carolina to see Grace and bring her presents.

It had been a bittersweet celebration. Grace missed her mom, but not like in the beginning. David missed her too, but the sharp, cutting pain he used to feel was gone - and had been since meeting Kristi. David hadn't said a word to Lydia's parents about Kristi - he hadn't had to; Grace said enough for both of them.

David had been worried they would be upset, but Lydia's mother had blown him away when she came to him and told him that she and her husband would support David if he ever decided to get married again. All they asked is that they still be allowed to be a part of Grace's life.

David hugged her and promised she and Lydia's father would always be welcome to see Grace. David had worked in his workshop while the three of them had gone to see the new Veggie Tales movie at the theater. Grace seemed to enjoy the attention and Lydia's father told him they had only had to avoid two reporters. Apparently word had gotten out that Grace could no longer heal.

He wondered what Kristi had done for the day. Grace pulled on his shirt and demanded, "Well?"

David squatted down beside her on the front step. It was a beautiful winter day. The sun shone warmly overhead and although there was a bit of a bite to the air, it was still a good day to be outside. The clouds chased each other while several birds scavenged for whatever they could find. He'd have to remember to fill the feeders today.

"I don't know, Grace. I'm working on it."

"Well, work faster. I miss her." Out of the mouths of babes.

"She lied to us Grace. I know you don't understand everything right now, but trust is a real big issue between a man and a woman."

"But she kept me safe; at least until the bad men got me. But that wasn't her fault. I left the room without telling you. Then she told you how to find me. That should count for something." The little girl crossed her arms across her chest and frowned at her father. Her lips were set in a mutinous expression that said she wasn't letting him off the hook that easy.

"It does, sweetie, it does."

"And besides, the Bible says to love your enemies, right?"

"Uh, yeah, yeah it does. Where did you get that anyway?"

"In Sunday School last Sunday. So anyway, I was thinking. If we're supposed to love our enemies, shouldn't we still love people who aren't our enemy, but maybe we're just kind of mad at? And besides, I'm not even mad at her. You are."

David wished he could keep up with her six-year-old mind. "I don't..."

But Grace wasn't finished with him, yet. "I mean think about it, Daddy. We're supposed to love people who do bad things – not the things they do, but the people themselves - but we can't love Kristi who did only one bad thing and a whole lot of good things? I mean like we've never done anything we needed forgiving for?" She rolled those blue eyes in exasperation with his stubborn refusal to forgive Kristi.

Before David could comment, Grace continued, "And if that's the case, then why do we need Jesus in the first place?" She stood, planted her hands on her hips and stamped a tiny foot. "Well, you and me both need Jesus because, well, because everyone does since everyone does wrong stuff that needs to be forgiven. He said so."

With a groan, David buried his head in his hands. How did you argue with six year old logic? And besides, she was absolutely right. He needed to forgive Kristi and move on.

Help, Lord. Although he figured his help had just been delivered in the form of his daughter. David had the feeling he had just heard the Lord speak through her mouth.

He threw his hands up in surrender. "Okay, I want to forgive her. I want to talk to her. I want to love her the rest of our lives. I just..." he stopped and shook his head.

"Here." Grace plopped the cordless phone in his hand. "It's ringing."

# # #

Kristi stepped on the pedal to open the trash can. The top flipped up, then stayed open. It was stuck again. She scraped the food into the can then turned on the hot water to rinse the plate. Eating alone had never been fun. Especially now when she wished she were sitting across from two sets of blue eyes.

Tess had come over last night to keep her company. She apologized again for her part in everything – unintentional as it was. Kristi had once again told her to put it behind her, but Tess was such a perfectionist, that even though Kristi had forgiven her, she would have a struggle forgiving herself – or trusting her judgment when it came to men and relationships in the future.

The only bright spot in the past two weeks had been Pamela's willingness to let her back into her life. Through Pamela, she had learned that David had dropped the charges against James. Apparently, as a father, knowing that James had no ulterior motive other than to have Grace heal his son had been easy for him to forgive.

Easier than forgiving her.

She put the plate in the dishwasher along with the fork. The empty TV dinner carton hit the trash can on the first toss; a fact that made her sad. She was getting too good at that particular toss. Always eating alone – and cleaning up alone.

Not to mention wallowing in self pity. Snap out of it, girl.

Kristi was also getting to know her nephew. Just in time to say good-bye. He was still unconscious, possibly even in a coma, but Pamela told her story after story about his life, letting Kristi see the mischievous side of his personality, yet letting her in on the compassionate nature he held for others.

She honestly didn't hold out for him to live more than a week or so. The respirator kept him breathing, the feeding tube kept him nourished. And the assortment of other drugs kept him alive. Postponing the inevitable. Her sister would lose a second child. Kristi had been shocked and saddened to hear the details of what had transpired once Pamela had left home.

Why hadn't Grace's prayer worked? Why didn't you heal him when she prayed, Lord?

Kristi knew God had a plan in everything; could even

use evil for His good. But she just couldn't see why God had seemed to ignore Grace's prayer this time. It was a question that plagued her if she thought about it too much. One that made her feel like there was unfinished business waiting for her. For Grace and David.

What do you have in mind, Lord?

The words from her morning devotion in proverbs chapter three flashed through her mind. "Trust in the Lord with all your heart. And lean not on your own understanding; In all your ways, acknowledge Him and He shall direct your paths."

She prayed aloud, "I'm trying Lord, I'm trying. Be with David. Strengthen him. Let him know I didn't mean to screw up so bad. Thanks for your forgiveness anyway. Maybe one day David will come to forgive me too."

The ringing of the phone distracted her from her prayer. Reporters probably. For the last two weeks, she had hidden out in her home avoiding any contact with the press. She had taken a leave of absence from MiracleCorp since she'd never been officially fired, until she could decide what to do with her life.

Kristi wandered over to check the caller I.D. box. Anonymous.

That meant it was an unlisted number. Should she pick it up? Ah well, at least it would force her out of her pity party mindset.

"Hello?" No one said anything. "Hello?"

"Ah, Kristi, hello."

It was David. Her entire body seemed to go numb and Kristi dropped the phone. In a flash, she scrambled to the floor to pick it up. Thank goodness the battery hadn't fallen out and disconnected him.

"David, hello. I, um, am surprised to hear your voice."

"I kind of got that idea when I heard the phone hit the floor." His voice was warm, but Kristi still shivered. Where was the anger? The bitterness?

"So how are you?" Kristi was desperate for some news of how he and Grace were doing. After spending so much time talking to him, sharing with him – loving him, the past two weeks had left an aching black hole in the vicinity of where her heart was supposed to beat.

"I'm better. Grace is fine. The resiliency of children and all that."

"Oh, I'm so glad she's okay."

"Yeah."

The conversation was stilted, neither of them knowing what to say, so Kristi took the plunge. "I've missed you, David. I don't know how to make everything up to you, but if I could do it all over again, I'd do it differently."

David's sigh blew through the wire. Kristi could just picture him running his hand through his hair. "I've missed you too, Kristi. Grace has too. In fact she's the reason we're talking. She dialed your number and handed me the phone."

Kristi let out a light laugh. "Remind me to give her a big hug when I see her. Assuming I'm going to get to see her sometime." She trailed off, praying for a positive response.

"I think that can be arranged. Mom's flying in this afternoon from Italy. Would you like to ride to the airport with us?"

"You bet I would." She couldn't keep the grin off her face or out of her voice.

"I gotta tell you, I'm just about caught up on all my work. Carpentry has always been 'thinking work', and it seems the more I thought, the more I worked and before I knew it, I had all these orders finished. And believe me, I was doing a lot of thinking. I've even almost finished the roof of my new barn. Anyway, we still have a lot to talk about, but I think I'm ready to do that if you are."

"Just tell me when."

"How about in an hour and a half?"

"I'll be waiting."

Kristi hung up the phone with the smile still spread across her face. He had called. And what's more, he wanted to talk. Thank you thank you thank you, Lord.

The next hour and a half were probably the slowest she'd ever lived through. She changed outfits twice before she settled on a pair of faded blue jeans and jade green sweater that made her eyes really stand out. A pair of comfortable boots completed the outfit. She left her hair down around her shoulders with the sides tucked behind her ears. A touch of lip gloss, and she was ready to go. Time dragged, but finally David's red explorer pulled into her driveway. An attack of nerves had her hands trembling as she pushed back a lock of hair that kept trying to dip into her eye. Maybe she should have clipped it back.

The doorbell rang and Kristi knew it was time. Lord, you know what I want. But more than that, I want what you want. Lead me where you would have me be. With David preferably, but if not, please show me how to deal with it.

She grabbed her coat from the back of the couch and was ready. A quick tug on the door had her standing face to face with the man she had come to love in such a short time.

"Hi," she breathed. He looked better than she remembered. He had on blue jeans too and a blue pull over fleece. He had his hands shoved in his pockets and his shoulders hunched against the chill. No coat, of course. His beautiful eyes reflected an inner peace. Thank you for that, Lord.

He smiled. "Hi yourself. How've you been?"

"Okay," she lied.

"Liar."

Kristi winced and David took her hand. "Hey, it was a joke." He sighed and added, "A bad one. It just popped out - no hidden meanings or intended sarcasm, I promise. Come on."

Kristi followed him to the car and got in. The back seat

was empty. "Where's Grace?"

"She staying with her mother's parents today. They called at the last minute and decided to drive down to see her. They try every couple of weeks or so to visit. Or, if I have a slow week and some time, I drive her up to see them."

So they would be alone for the thirty-minute drive to the airport. That could be a good thing, although Kristi had planned on the having the little girl around to use as a distraction if she needed one. She adjusted the seat belt while she thought of how to begin.

"So, you want to start?" David questioned.

A small laugh bubbled out before she could catch it. "You're still doing it, Walton."

"Yeah, I figured I'd go ahead and break the ice."

"Consider it broken. Okay, I'll start. I'm really surprised you called. What made you decide you weren't angry with me anymore?"

"A six-year old with too much wisdom for her own good, but just enough for her dear old dad."

"Ahhh. Explanation please?"

David shrugged. "It was really a matter of choice. I could be mad at you and unforgiving and be miserable the rest of my life or I could forgive you and we could move on. Besides, I'm a man of God now and God commands us to forgive."

Kristi wasn't sure if she liked that explanation or not. But David wasn't finished. "I also realized that my feelings for you went beyond friendship. I missed you. I wanted to forgive you and believe you. I know you, Kristi." David stopped talking long enough to pull the car over to the side of the road. Mullhaven Park was right there. "Come with me. Mom's plane won't land for another hour or so." David climbed out of the car without giving her time to answer or question where he was going. Kristi followed. He took her hand and walked silently beside her.

Sounds like the flag whipping in the wind and cars passing on the highway faded to the background as David pulled her to a stop. The duck pond was frozen, but Kristi felt warm all over when David put his arm around her and tucked her into his side.

"What do you mean you know me?" She was a little nervous; butterflies were having a field day inside her stomach.

David turned her so that her arms were trapped against his chest. His wrapped her tight and his forehead dropped to hers. He looked straight into her eyes, holding her captive. "I know you. It's that simple. We spent so much time together while we were on the road. Granted, it wasn't all fun and games, but you must admit, we spent the majority of that time talking and getting to know each other."

"True." Kristi shivered, but not necessarily from the cold.

"As I said before, I spent a lot the last two weeks thinking."

"Uh huh."

Every time he spoke, his warm breath brushed her cheek. It smelled like wintergreen. She had noticed the bag of mints on the back seat. Kristi thought for the umpteenth time about what nice lips he had.

"And," he paused and Kristi fairly shouted at him to hurry up; instead she bit her lip, "and, I decided that there was no way I didn't see your true personality, your integrity and passion for God. None of that could have been a show. You have honest eyes."

"But I still lied to you, David." The pain of her deception still ached when she thought about it too long.

"Yes, by omission mostly. But your motives were pure. Not that that excuses it or makes it all right, but you weren't out to hurt us or to gain something for yourself."

"Well, that's not entirely true."

David frowned, "What do you mean?"

"I knew I needed to tell you everything, that's true. But I was afraid if I did, I'd lose you. Which is crazy since I never had you in the first place."

David's frown turned to a tender smile and his lips lightly touched the end of her nose. "Oh yes you did. From the moment we shook hands in the cemetery, you captured a part of my heart. Definitely my interest. I couldn't stop thinking about you."

That confession made Kristi's heart soar. "Really?"

"Yes, now hush and let me finish."

She snapped her mouth shut.

"Thank you." He gave her another squeeze. "You showed me who you were in so many different ways. Like, the way you tried to save Grace the morning she was snatched." His fingers ran down the cheek she had scraped so badly. It was almost healed now, but she would have some slight scarring from the ordeal. Nothing that makeup wouldn't hide, though. "And later, I realized the whole reason you were looking for who was behind everything at MiracleCorp was to reunite with your sister. To prove her husband innocent."

"Oh David. I wish I'd done it all different."

"And the fact that you wish you'd done it all different. You're a wonderful, caring, sweet person, who gives all she's got to those she cares about."

Kristi shifted, a little uncomfortable with the praise she didn't feel like she deserved. "Thank you."

"I want to keep seeing you, Kristi. I've fallen in love with you and I can't fight it anymore. I'm absolutely miserable without you."

The words she had most wanted to hear now left her virtually speechless. But in the next moment, she didn't need any words as his head tilted a fraction and his warm lips closed over hers. It was a sweet questing kiss that spoke of promises to come. A future together. And it ended far too soon.

When he pulled away, Kristi's hands slid up to cup his cheeks. "I love you, David Walton. I would move heaven and earth to spend more time with you." She gave a small laugh. "And time I've got as I'm no longer employed."

#

David grinned down at her absolutely amazed that this incredible woman loved him. "We can fix that. There's always an opening for a good doctor in town – even a famous one like yourself."

Kristi grimaced, then gave a wry grin. "Don't you mean infamous?"

"Hm, that may be a more accurate description."

She lightly pinched his cheek. "Smart aleck."

David dropped another kiss on her lips, then started pulling her back toward the car. "Come on. Mom's plane should be arriving any moment now."

Kristi smiled all the way to the airport. David couldn't keep the grin off his face either.

David found a parking spot and he and Kristi made their way to baggage claim where he had made arrangements to meet his mother. Kristi asked, "What do you think your mother's going to think about us?" She tugged on the hem of her sweater.

David grinned down at her, "She's going to be thrilled, trust me." Then he sobered and pulled her to a stop at the baggage claim. The plane had just landed, but the passengers had yet to get off the plane. "Kristi..."

His sober tone brought a frown to Kristi's face. "What is it?" she asked warily.

"Lydia would have chosen you."

Tears formed and Kristi choked them back. She no longer felt like she was in competition with a ghost. David had made his peace. "Thanks, David."

He went on, "I'll always have my memories of Lydia, good memories, memories I'll want to share with Grace." Kristi swallowed hard and David could see that she wondered where he was going with this. "But," he smiled as he reached out and scraped a knuckle gently down her cheek, "you and I, we'll make our own memories. Ones that we'll get to tell our grandkids about. Deal?"

Kristi nodded. She couldn't speak past the lump in her throat.

"David? Kristi?"

The two turned as one to see David's mother heading their way. She had a beautiful smile on her face. When she reached them, she enveloped both in a crushing bear hug and said, "Oh, it is so good to see you two. I've missed you, son, and Grace. I am so glad she's okay."

"She's great mom. She can't wait to see you and hear all about your trip." The baggage roller started humming, then moving. "Let's get your bag, and get going."

Finally, the right bag appeared from under the curtain and David grabbed it and slung it over his shoulder. Nancy had left in such a hurry, she'd only had the one small bag.

David looked at the women and asked, "Ready?" They nodded and the three started walking towards the exit, David on one side of his mother, Kristi on the other. The woman gripped Kristi arm, then looked up at David with a mischievous smile. "So, when's the wedding?"

Heads turned to watch with amusement at the three people laughing hysterically and many wondered why the younger woman's face had turned such an interesting shade of red.

Chapter 15

David pounded another nail into the barn roof he was finishing up. It would be his new work/storage building - at least until Grace talked him into the horse she kept bugging him about - although come to think of it, she hadn't said much about it lately. Maybe the horse phase had finally passed. He was glad he had bought two lots when the neighborhood had been going up. Instead of selling the property next door for a profit as originally planned, he had kept it.

Now Grace had a huge backyard to play in and he had enough room that he didn't feel like he was elbow to elbow with his neighbors. It had been two weeks since his and Kristi's rendezvous in the park. Two weeks of smiles and laughter; giggles and picnics that left them shivering in the cold. David wouldn't have changed a moment even if he could have.

A car pulled into the drive. He looked up – and smiled. Kristi was here. David heard the storm door slam and knew Grace was bolting for the car. The little girl had blossomed under the attention Kristi showered upon her. Kristi seemed to enjoy her time with Grace just as much. David's heart swelled with love and thanksgiving. Thank you God for sending her into our lives. I don't always understand your ways or your methods, but thanks just the same.

One more nail and he would take a break and go greet

his girls. On the downswing of the hammer, Grace gave a screaming laugh and David looked up to see Kristi tickling Grace's ribs. In that split second, the hammer continued down and hit his thumb with force. Blood spurted. His arm jerked in reflex at the excruciating pain, which in turn caused his foot to slip on the sloping roof.

After that everything seemed to happen in slow motion. One moment he was looking at blue sky, the next he felt a sharp, searing, mind-numbing pain at the base of his skull, then nothing - but he was still conscious. He lay on the ground gasping for breath. His head swam; the darkness closed in.

Don't pass out; you've got to get help.

"David!" Kristi's terrified scream told him that help was on the way. His breath was slowing coming back to his lungs. Funny, he didn't feel any pain. Even his thumb didn't hurt anymore.

Kristi reached his side, tears running freely down her ashen cheeks. "David, what happened? Tell me where it hurts." Her professional doctor's hands ran over his body; feeling here, poking there. "Does it hurt when I do this?"

"Do what?" He couldn't feel a thing. Dread churned inside him.

"David," her voice was a whisper as realization dawned in her green eyes. "What about here?"

David closed his eyes and swallowed hard; he coughed. "Nothing."

Kristi began to weep in earnest. "I think you're back is broken. I'll get your mother to call an ambulance. Hold on, David, just hold on. You're going to be fine."

He had broken his back. Fear was a living creature, crawling, and writhing its way through his now helpless body. God, help me!

"Daddy?" Grace's soft voice cut into his silent plea. Concern and fear clouded her eyes. Tears trembled on her lashes.

"Hi baby, Daddy's going to be all right. You go on back inside and stay with Granma, okay?" He was having trouble talking now. Breathing was an effort. Blood pooled in his mouth, then out and down the side of his face. He choked; coughed again. He must have a punctured lung.

"Grace, go inside, okay? Help is on the way." Kristi was back. But she was fading. He thought he felt her hand wipe away the blood.

"I love you, Grace."

"...love...too, Daddy." He felt her small hand touch his face. Her voice came from far away. Sounds were muted. The blue sky faded to gray.

"...Jesus...heal...Daddy. He's hurt and needs your help. Could you please just help him get better and fix his bones? Kristi said his back was broken. Please, Jesus, make him all better. Amen."

David's whole body felt like it was on fire - but it didn't hurt. It burned, then tingled. David then felt the sweetest rush of - love? pulse through him, filling every pore, every crevice of his heart and soul. Then nothing.

Awareness was instant. Breathing had never felt so good. He sat up. Grace's joyous laughter turned him in her direction. She was hugging her stomach and had a huge grin on her face. She giggled, laughed, and jumped up and down like she couldn't contain her joy.

David focused back on himself. There was no pain. He stood, then jumped up and down, imitating Grace's movements. His laughter joined with Grace's. Kristi was staring at them wide-eyed, then she too, began to laugh. She launched herself into his arms, tears of joy streaking her cheeks in place of the previous tears of fear and heartache.

"David, He healed you, He really did!"

Thank you, God! These were the only words David could form in his mind at the moment. Thank you, God!

David blinked. Things were fuzzy. He couldn't see

straight.

What in the world? Had God healed him only to give him blurry vision?

"What wrong, David?" Kristi paused between breaths of laughter to question him.

"I can't see. Everything's fuzzy." He rubbed his eyes and the gritty feel of the contacts rubbing under his lids made him laugh. "My contacts."

"Take them out, David. I bet you don't need them anymore."

David reached up with forefinger and thumb to grasp the tiny item and pull it from his left eye. He blinked then did the same with the right eye. His eyes darted all around and then a big booming laugh bellowed from the pit of his stomach. "He healed those too!"

Kristi and Grace joined him once again in uproarious laugher and the three hugged once again.

"What's going on?" David's mother stared at the three of them in shock. "Kristi said you fell of the roof. I called an ambulance. What happened? Are you all right?"

David grabbed her in a bear hug and swung her around. She looked at him like he'd lost his mind. He laughed again. "I did, Mom. I was lying on the ground, the life draining right out of me. Grace prayed for me and God healed me. Eyes, thumb, back, and everything. Simple as that."

The woman looked shell shocked at first, then she started smiling. "Well, praise the Lord."

"Yes indeed, praise the Lord."

She started backing toward the house once David set her back on the ground. "I'll just go cancel the ambulance." David heard her still praising the Lord as she hurried to make the call.

"Daddy, I need you to take me somewhere fast."

David stooped to her level, still full of joy and reveling

in the miraculous. "Where do you need to go, Grace?"

"I need you to take me to see Seth Sinclair."

#

James stood beside the bed watching his son die. Heartbreak didn't begin to describe what he was feeling. He had done all he could possibly – humanly, do and now there was nothing left to do. He had all the medical care money could buy, but it made no difference to Seth.

Seth had actually lived longer than expected. The doctor's couldn't tell him how Seth was still hanging on to life. But now, it was time. He had taken a turn for the worse. His son was all but gone.

"He's just about gone, isn't he?" Pamela's words brought his head up. She stood in the door, her shoulder braced against the door jam as though standing required too much energy. James walked over to her and put his arms around her. He leaned down to kiss her forehead. Words wouldn't come. He just held her.

"You've changed, James."

He opened his eyes and looked down into Pamela's. "What do you mean?"

She lifted a shoulder in small shrug and said, "You're just different. It's hard to explain. I think all that Bible reading and praying has done something inside you."

James realized she was right. "Yes, I think you're right." He gave a humorless laugh. "I've certainly realized that money doesn't buy everything and that as powerful as I foolishly believed I was, my power has its limits. There's definitely Someone more powerful than I am." He shut his eyes again and said, "He's going to die, Pammie and I'm going to need you."

Resignation, despair, sheer depression settled on him like an anchor; the weight so heavy surely it would slowly crush him. He opened his eyes again and the look on Pamela's face floored him.

Tears chased one another down her hollow cheeks, but hope blazed in her eyes replacing the deadness that had been there for what seemed like forever. She choked, "I've waited a long time for those words, James. I love you and I'll be here. We'll get through it together."

He'd forgotten how it felt to lean on someone else. It felt good. Pamela gave him a brief kiss, then walked over to Seth and placed soft kiss on his ashen face. He already looked dead. Pamela left the room and James returned to his silent grief. He did now have hope that their marriage would survive when Seth died. But there was something else missing. Something James couldn't quite put his finger on.

He knew dark circles rung his eyes; clothes hung on his now slender frame. The nurse had been sent home. Brain activity still registered, but nothing else. Seth didn't even respond to the touch of a hand or a kiss on the forehead. The respirator still pumped and whooshed in its endless rhythm. A touch of a switch, a flick of his finger, and that too would cease.

James knew that even with the machines still on, it wouldn't be long before the brain activity would stop and his son would be technically, medically dead. Then he would turn the switch off and Seth would be physically gone.

But gone where? Where would he go when he died? Kristi had explained heaven and hell to him when he'd asked her that question. It matched what he'd been reading in the Bible. Did Seth believe? Kristi said the first time she'd spent time with Seth, she'd gone through what she called the plan of salvation. She'd prayed a prayer and told Seth that if he wanted that to be his prayer to squeeze her hand. Kristi said she'd felt a faint, almost non-existent pressure, but she'd felt it.

So did that mean Seth would be in heaven when he died?

Kristi had said he would. James looked up at the ceiling and spoke his prayer out loud. "God are you there? I believe you exist; I've read your Word. I want to be with Seth – and you -when I die. Tell me what to do. This time I'm asking you. Please, please spare my son. But if you decide not to, tell me how to be with him when I die. I can't command you, I can't order you, I can only ask. I'm not used to asking for anything, but this time, it's out of my hands and in yours."

"James?"

James didn't even realize the tears were on his cheeks or that he'd dropped to his knees until he heard a noise in the doorway and he looked up to see David and Grace Walton standing there. Kristi was right behind them.

He was so surprised he just stared at the little girl. She shifted on her feet as though unsure what to do next. "Hello, Grace. Would you like to come in and visit Seth?"

Grace slowly let go of the death grip she had on her father's hand and sidled up to Seth's bedside. Her small hand reached out to pick up Seth's and her eyes rose to meet his.

James wasn't sure what to say to her, so he addressed her father. "Ah, thank you for coming."

"We had to."

James was puzzled by that response, but said nothing.

"God didn't heal him last time." Grace spoke quietly, but firmly.

James cleared his throat and focused back on the little girl. "No, no he didn't. I haven't had the chance to tell you, but I owe you an apology, Grace. I never should have done what I did, and I'm really, really sorry. I hope one day you'll be able to forgive me."

A small smile crept across her lips and any remaining fear that she may have felt in his presence seemed to fade away. "I forgive you."

At her innocent and ready forgiveness, a lump formed in his throat. After all he had done to her, she offered him the gift of her instant forgiveness. James was overwhelmed.

Did God forgive that easily? Could it really be that simple? If he apologized to God, would God simply say, "I forgive you.?"

"Thank you, Grace. You don't know what that means to me. I've asked God why He didn't heal Seth before when you were here and I don't have an answer, but maybe I'm just not meant to know that now."

"I don't know either. I asked God to take away His gift so the bad men would leave us alone. I thought maybe that's why He didn't heal Seth, but then later I thought maybe it was because you just didn't ask Him to."

Stunned at her answer, he saw that it was exactly the revelation that he had come to when he realized that he couldn't command God to do anything.

"Ask Him." Pamela's voice came to him from behind David.

"What?"

"Well, it can't hurt, can it?" There was no sarcasm, no hint of derision that usually accompanied her words when she spoke about God. She was slowly coming around. Maybe one day…

"No, no it can't." He turned to Grace. "Do you think He would listen?"

Grace laughed, but James didn't take offense. She assured him, "Of course He would listen. He always listens. Sometimes He says no, though when you ask Him for something. I've been asking him for a horse for three years now."

James didn't know whether to laugh or cry at her earnest statement. Oh, to have the relationship with the Almighty that this child had. Excitement grew inside him at the thought.

"Okay, I'll ask Him." James bowed his head and right there in front of everybody cried out to the One who loved him unconditionally. "God, I don't know what to say except

I'm sorry for my arrogance, my assumptions that I could order you to do my will, when I should have been asking you for guidance. I've read a lot in your Word, you've revealed yourself to me through that and through this little girl and her father. I'm asking you to forgive me and to show me how to live from here on out. If you could see to using Grace to heal Seth, I would be eternally grateful. If not, then give me the strength to deal with it. Thank you."

His voice was shaking by the time he finished, but his heart felt lighter than it has in years.

Grace's prayer followed his. "Jesus, Seth is real sick and needs you to heal him. I know you love him and want what's best for him, but if you could leave him here a little longer, his mommy and daddy would be so happy. Thank you, Jesus. Amen."

# # #

The next few moments would be written upon her memory for the rest of her life. Kristi would never forget what happened after Grace's simple and heartfelt prayer. Seth's eyes opened. In the blink of an eye, his frail frame gained thirty pounds. Color flooded into his cheeks and he stared in wonder at the people gathered around his bed. The respirator still pumped and Kristi knew he had no more use for it.

Grace giggled in glee and with a joy that she seemed to feel each time this happened.

Shaking, Kristi forced herself into doctor mode and instructed Seth in what to do so she could remove the tube from his throat, the feeding tube from his nose, the IV from his arm and the wires attached to his head.

When he was disconnected from everything, he sat up. "Dad?"

James was prostrate on the floor, weeping uncontrollably. At Seth's voice, he stood and stumbled to sit on the bed next to his healthy, fully healed son. Pamela stood staring in complete and total shock.

"Mom? What's going on? Hey! I feel great – and hungry. Got anything to eat around here?"

He grinned at his parents and Kristi's heart melted at the sight. He was adorable. He looked like Pamela, but with a devilish gleam in his eyes and two killer dimples.

Kristi reached for his hand and gave it a squeeze. "Hi, Seth. I'm your Aunt Kristi."

"Hey, I remember you. Only I thought you were in my dream. You told me about God and heaven."

"Yes," Kristi spoke around the lump in her throat, "yes, I did. I thought you heard me."

"I heard. I also felt really peaceful, like everything was gonna be okay no matter what. I heard Dad praying, then a little girl praying, then all of a sudden, I felt like I was on fire, only it didn't hurt. Then I woke up to see all of you."

Pamela had her arms around him by this time. James had his arms around the both of them. Seth's next words were muffled by all of the embraces. "So, what does a guy have to do to get some food around here?"

Kristi laughed around her hiccups. What an incredible God He was. Kristi pulled Grace to her and hugged her. "You are such a special little girl. I hope you know that even if God didn't use you this way, you'd still be special. You know that, right?"

Grace just grinned up at her, joy radiating from her slight frame. "I know God might not heal every time I pray, but it sure is awesome when He does, isn't it?"

"It sure is."

"I still want to be a doctor like you." Grace flashed her another impish grin and Kristi laughed and gave her another tight squeeze.

James finally got control of his emotions and walked over to Grace to lean down and stare into her eyes. "That's some gift you've got there, little girl."

"God gave it to me."

"I know."

Kristi spoke up. "I think you got the greatest gift of all today, James."

"I sure did. I got my son back."

"No, you got something even greater than that."

Everyone looked over at Kristi waiting for her to explain that statement. After all, what could be greater than Seth being healed?

"You know, God offers all kinds of blessings and gifts. One of those being, 'For God so loved the world that He gave his only begotten son, that whosoever believeth in him should not perish, but have everlasting life.' Some people reject that gift, but not you, James. You received the most priceless gift God has to offer."

A light was beginning to shine in James' eyes. David walked over and slid his arm around Kristi's shoulder to give a tight squeeze. He nodded his understanding.

Grace grinned, clasped her hands under her chin and bounced on her toes. Seth held his mother's hand while Pamela waited for Kristi to reveal exactly what it was that James had received.

Kristi smiled through her tears. " 'For by grace you are saved through faith and that not of yourselves; it is the gift of God.' You, James Sinclair have received eternal life with Him through His only son, Jesus Christ, God's true gift of Grace."

Printed in the United States
24600LVS00002B/64-264

9 781594 679278